To Ila,

William J. "Bill" Kelly

Buck's War

by
William F. Kelly

authorHOUSE™

1663 LIBERTY DRIVE, SUITE 200
BLOOMINGTON, INDIANA 47403
(800) 839-8640
WWW.AUTHORHOUSE.COM

First published by AuthorHouse 09/29/05

ISBN: 1-4208-6481-5 (sc)
ISBN: 1-4208-7638-4 (dj)

Library of Congress Control Number: 2005905439

Printed in the United States of America
Bloomington, Indiana

This book is printed on acid-free paper.

Dedication

My love, appreciation and thanks to Polly
for her support, suggestions and help.

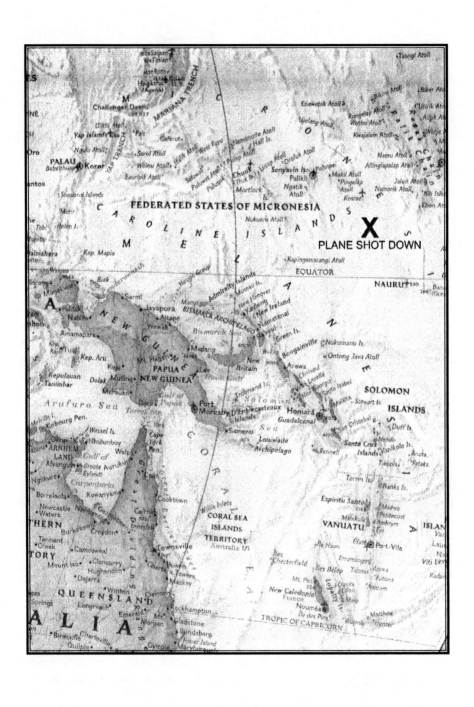

Buck's Island

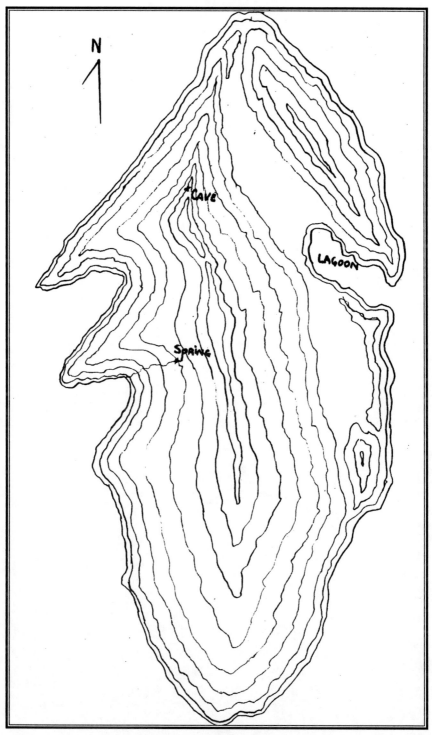

Chapter 1

Spring came and passed quickly on Long Island. The winter was cold and the early spring was wet. Then on the first week of May the temperature abruptly turned to summer. Buck was sitting in the classroom trying to pay attention to his English teacher, Mrs. Shumway, who was reciting one of Shakespeare's sonnets. His mind, however, refused to cooperate. It kept returning to his decision. Since the Japanese had attacked Pearl Harbor he had been thinking about the war almost exclusively and what his role should be.

The birds were singing outside the open windows of Mineola High School and the trees were almost in full bloom, sprinkling their pollen everywhere. The crabapple trees were putting on quite a show and the dogwood on some streets were breathtaking. It was time to be in love but Buck's heart just wasn't in it. His thoughts were of the war and when he should join. Other guys talked about enlisting after graduation but they were also making plans for summer jobs and for the Fourth of July. Buck doubted their sincerity.

Alice bumped into Buck on purpose as they met at their lockers.

"Why so glum, chum?"

"Oh, hi, Alice. I guess you caught me daydreaming."

"Anything the matter? How did you do on the Math test?"

"I did great." After a moment's hesitation he continued, "My mind was on what will happen after graduation. I can hardly listen to the news without thinking that I should be involved."

Alice and Buck closed their lockers and walked toward the gymnasium. They were a good looking couple. Alice was fair and blonde about five

1

foot five and Buck had an olive complexion, had brown hair and was just under six feet tall. They were both good students although Alice got better grades.

Buck had baseball practice and Alice would sit and watch and do some of her homework in the bleachers on nice days. And today was a nice day. Buck played center field because he had a great arm and he averaged over .325 at the plate. He most often batted cleanup but sometimes he would hit third or fifth if one of his teammates was hot. He was offered a scholarship to play baseball at Princeton but was now concerned that he might not even go to college.

After practice they would walk the two miles home. Alice lived just four blocks from Buck in the village of Williston Park, a mile north of Mineola and about twenty miles from New York City. The town was a bedroom community for "the Big Apple."

They found they liked each other the past summer when Alice visited the A&P grocery store where Buck worked. He helped her find some spices that were misplaced on the shelf and they started dating after school started in September. Then on December 7, 1941 the Japanese attack on Pearl Harbor changed everything.

On the walk home Buck told Alice what he was thinking.

"Alice, I think I'll enlist right after graduation."

"But why, Buck? They're not drafting eighteen year olds."

"Not yet. But I keep thinking I should be there fighting. I think of nothing else. I can hardly sleep. I don't care if the baseball team wins or loses and school has turned into a chore. It didn't even bother me when they cancelled the senior prom. Nothing seems to matter except defeating the Germans and the Japs."

"What about us, Buck? If you sign up we'll be separated, probably for a long time."

"Alice, I'm not going to like that. We're just starting to know each other and trust each other. I'm going to miss you."

"Then why not wait until you're called?" she questioned.

"If it would make a difference by waiting, I would wait," Buck explained. "But I feel like I'm only postponing the inevitable. They'll be calling eighteen year olds soon."

"But even a few months over the summer would be nice, wouldn't it?"

"Yes, but once I'm drafted I'll be just like everyone else who doesn't want to go to war. If I enlist I'll have some say in my assignment, maybe even being able to choose what I'm good at and want to do."

"I hate to think of you going to war, Buck. You'll probably think differently about it in a few weeks as we get closer to graduation."

"I doubt it. Just last week the Japanese captured the Philippines. My mother's family live in Manila. That means my grandmother, my uncle and two aunts are under the control of the Japanese. I can't imagine that. Maybe by enlisting I'll help bring the end of this war just a few days nearer."

"Have you spoken with your Dad and Mom?"

"Only about the war in general. My Mom is concerned about me but doesn't worry about Bobby because he's only fourteen. And Mickey is twelve and a girl and she won't have to go. Dad did mention that it would be a lot better to enlist than to wait for the draft to get me. He told me he would listen at work for any rumors about the draft as a lot of guys at work have sons my age. Right now Mom's hoping to get a letter from her family in Manila telling her that they're fine but I don't think she's going to hear anything until the Philippines are free."

They continued their conversation, covering school, friends, family and their future. At Remsen Street Buck said goodbye and continued walking the four blocks home. Since it was daylight saving time and would be until the end of the war, kids were out playing in the street. Henry Street seemed to have an extra number of kids and the street was the playground. This was going to be something he would miss even if he was too old to join in the games. The sounds of kids playing and having fun was always pleasant.

After supper his mother asked Buck why he wasn't eating.

"Martin, what's wrong with my spaghetti?"

"Mom, the spaghetti's fine. I'm just kind of lost in what I should be doing after graduation."

"I thought you would be taking that baseball scholarship to Princeton. Didn't you like the campus when you visited?"

"Yeah, it was great. But now I'm not sure I'll be going to college. At least until after the war. Dad, you said that it would be better to enlist than to be drafted and I know I don't want to be considered one of those who was forced to serve. I keep thinking I should be there now and I want to be doing something that will really help the war effort."

"Buck," said his father, "You have to finish high school. I can understand that maybe now's not the time to be going to college but you have to finish high school," he said emphatically.

"Dad, I know. I will graduate but I'm leaning toward enlisting in the marines right after that."

"Why the marines?" asked Bobby.

"Because they're tough and have great pride in what they do. Their motto is 'always faithful' and they take care of each other."

"They've got neat uniforms, too," said Mickey. "There was a marine waiting outside of school this week and he really was spiffy."

"Martin, let your Dad and I talk about it a bit. Maybe we'll have some more thoughts about what would be best. We know it's your life but your leaving will effect the whole family. Just don't do anything hasty until we talk it over."

"Sure, Mom. I want your blessing and your permission." With a wink he added, "I don't need it but I want it anyway."

Buck was known by several names. He was baptized Martin Joseph and his mother often called him Martin. But to keep the confusion to a minimum with two Martins in the house, young Martin was called Son and eventually Sonny. When he went to school the children knew and loved the popular movie idol, Buck Jones, and thought it was clever to call Martin, "Buck." It stuck and no one thought to call him anything else, except his Mom.

The meal was finished and Martin sat down in the living room to read the afternoon paper. Mickey, whose real name was Maryann, went into the kitchen to help her mother with the dishes and Bobby and Buck went outside to toss the baseball around for a few minutes. Bobby saw Buck's enlisting as a great adventure, a chance to see the world and get a few licks in at the enemy. Buck didn't try to convince him otherwise. Let him think that I'm the luckiest guy in the world, was Buck's thought.

Chapter 2

Helena Jones was born in the Philippines and met Martin when he was stationed there in 1918 at the end of World War I. Martin enlisted in the Army and the war came to a close so they shipped him to Manila. There he was assigned to a Military Police unit. He met Lena at the Army mess where she worked serving food. Her mother also worked there in the kitchen as a cook. She was efficient, friendly and anticipated your needs before you knew you needed something. She was sixteen when Martin first met her and after two years he asked her to go to a dance at the local Catholic Church. She said that she would like that but would need to check with her mother first. Mrs. Alvarez liked Martin and gave her daughter permission. In several months Martin sought out the Catholic Chaplain to ask what he needed to do to marry Lena since both were Catholic and if he would be able to bring her with him when he returned home. With the help of the Chaplain they got married in Manila and Lena came to the States with him when his tour was over. She took several trips back to visit her family but knew that the war would make visits impossible. She only hoped that her family was safe.

Lena sat in her rocking chair after breakfast was over. The kids were off to school and Martin was long gone to work. He was usually up at five and on his way about forty-five minutes later. As a detective with the Mineola Police Department he had a lot of freedom to make his own hours but was usually at his desk at six and home by three in the afternoon. The exception was when he was working on a case that required him to stay later.

Lena spent the first minutes of every day in prayer. She sat in the rocker and offered up to God, "all the prayers, works and sufferings of the day," as she learned long ago in convent school. She would then talk to God in her own words. Sometimes she would just listen, but usually she had some thoughts that needed to be expressed. These prayer sessions would be as short as ten minutes or as long as a half hour but Lena never paid attention to the time when she was conversing with God. First she told God that she was concerned about her mother, brother and sisters and her aunts and uncles in the Philippines. She asked God to watch over them and also to watch over Buck. She didn't realize that she was speaking out loud. "He's going to join the marines and I want you to care for him. Please. I'll let him go but you must take care of him," was her prayer. Then she sat there in quiet and listened. After a while she said out loud, "Thank you," blessed herself and started her work day.

From the rocker to the kitchen, the bedrooms and straightening up around the house in general was Lena's usual plan. And like most of the women in the neighborhood she assigned certain chores to specific days. Monday was for washing, Tuesday for shopping, Wednesday for dusting, mopping and vacuuming and Thursday for ironing. But her love was to spend time in the garden and work with her flowers and when the weather in the spring turned nice like today, she would find time to be outdoors. Even when she was turning the soil to make a new bed for flowers her thoughts kept coming back to Buck and his decision to join the marines. She knew he had to go and she was so proud of him wanting to go and serve. This country had been good to her and her family and she wanted to give back to it for all she had received. But she didn't want it to be with the life of her firstborn. But she had to tell Buck that he had her blessing and his father's as well.

She continued working outside, realizing that she was still in prayer. She remembered in a sermon that one saint had said "To labor is to pray." She had always felt that her work was a form of prayer and that work in the garden was especially prayerful. Between the chores and work in the garden the day went quickly and Mickey and Bobby were home shortly after three. Martin was home a half hour later and said that he was going to work out in the garage. He had a punching bag and speed bag set up in the garage and used the garage to exercise and stay in shape. He had boxed in the army and liked to skip rope, and hit the bags. He was six feet tall and solidly built with a tendency to put on a few pounds in the middle. Lena was pleased with her husband keeping in shape and watching his weight. She thought he had a nice build at twenty-one and now at forty-five he was still good looking.

Mickey changed clothes and joined the other kids outside. Sometimes they played at the school playground which was just up the block but usually they played in the street. All kinds of ball games were played with rules adjusted for when young kids were playing or more girls than boys. When the girls played jump rope the boys would also take a turn. They usually didn't like the tricky stuff and told the girls not to say those dumb rhymes but they could usually hold their own and stay jumping for a good time. The girls were invited to play the kickball games and 'mud-gutter' and usually initiated the choice of hide-and-seek and ring-a-leavio. There was always something going on in the street and since hardly any cars came down the street it was more often than not the playground of choice for the kids. Parents liked having the children where they could see them and knew they were safe. The sound of children playing in the street was one of the happy memories of childhood.

Bobby played stoop ball for a while with a neighbor but when the neighbor was called in he decided to get started on his homework. In just a few more weeks school would be out and he could forget homework for a while. Bobby was a better than average student but not as good as Buck. At least that is what the teachers would tell him. It made him angry that teachers would make those stupid comparisons since he was a better all around athlete than Buck. But Bobby had to admit that Buck was a great baseball player and had great stamina especially for long distance running events. And he was strong although Bobby figured he would probably be stronger when he was eighteen. He remembered that his Dad would tell him that everyone had talents and it was his responsibility to develop and use the talents that God gave us.

There was no comparison between Bobby and Mickey since she was a girl and two years younger. But there wasn't a twelve year old girl who came near to being as fast, strong or athletic as Mickey. She epitomized the name, "tomboy."

After supper, while they were still at the table, Lena told Buck that she and his Dad had talked and would give him their blessing for joining the marines. They were glad that he was waiting until after graduation and they told him that they were proud of what he wanted to do. His Dad told him that beating the crowd would be helpful and he would probably get special attention.

"Keep your eyes out for things you like to do and maybe can do after the war. I have a friend who started radio in the army and makes his living repairing radios today. I was an MP in the army and am a policeman today. The army prepared me for that job," said Martin.

After supper Lena and Martin sat down at the kitchen table to organize the ration books and to figure out what they could buy. The blue stamps allowed you to buy fruits and vegetables and the red stamps meat and cheese. Each amount and quality of meat required so many points and you had to have stamps in order to buy those foods. Very often, especially with meats, you couldn't buy what you wanted and waited in line for an hour to buy, even though you had the stamps. Lena was good about finding the best buys. She knew when to shop and was always nice to Johnny, the butcher, long before the war started. He didn't forget her kindnesses.

Gas rationing had started earlier in the year but only now, in May, did rationing of fuel get serious. The general population had been allowed to buy four gallons of gas a week but was now reduced to two and a half gallons. Those essential to the war effort and the public safety and welfare were allocated what was needed. This included the police. Children and some adults used their bicycles and everyone walked or took public transportation. It was an inconvenience but most people felt that when compared with those doing the fighting it was insignificant.

That night as they were each getting ready for bed, Bobby asked Buck if he was scared.

"Sure, Bobby, I'm scared. Most of all I'm scared of the unknown. I don't know where I'll be going, what I'll be doing or how close to the enemy I'll get. I don't know whether I'll be fired at or not or whether I'll have to kill the enemy. I'll just have to take it as it comes."

"I'll be thinking of you every day and I'll pray for you every night," was Bobby's response.

"Thanks, Bobby. I'll be counting on it," Buck said as he turned off the light on the stand next to his bed.

Chapter 3

It was the first week in June when the 'dim outs' began. All cars had to cover the upper half of their headlights with black tape so that the light would only shine down and houses had to be equipped with shades that didn't allow light to show out. They had several drills in which the fire siren would sound and all houses had to be dark and show no light. Mr. Kelly was the block warden and it was his responsibility to make certain that no home showed any light. He would walk the street and knock on the door of any house that showed even the slightest sliver of light. It was amazing how dark the neighborhood would get a minute after the siren would blow. Because Long Island stuck out in the Atlantic Ocean and was so close to New York Harbor, sightings of U-boats were often reported. There was even a rumor that a U-boat dropped saboteurs off on the beach on the south shore of the island. In any case, getting people to cooperate was no problem.

Bobby and Mickey were involved in saving newspapers, vegetable cans, aluminum foil, tooth paste containers and scrap metal. Martin got a box in the garage for them to put all but the newspapers. They would be wrapped with string and the Kelly kids down the street would haul them in their wagon to the school on certain days.

Buck continued to play baseball and got ready for his final high school exams, known as the Regents. They were administered at the same time and on the same day throughout the state and were feared by almost all students. They were usually fair but tough. It would be foolish not to study for the Regents. He was a very good student at Math, good in History and

Science and average in English. It was the English that he needed to study the most and that was the subject that he disliked to study.

He continued to see Alice, mainly at school. Occasionally in the evening he would walk the four blocks to her house and they would sit on the front steps and talk. They both felt that time was running out for them. And it was.

Buck had talked with a recruiter, filled out an application, took some tests and had already heard that he was accepted for boot camp after graduation. Graduation was on a Friday evening, June 26th and he was expected to meet in the main lobby of Pennsylvania Station on July 6th, the Monday after the Independence Day holiday. Now that it was June, he had to tell Alice that he would be leaving just a week after graduation.

"I know, Buck. It's what you have to do. I even understand all of that.... but I don't have to like it."

"If I don't do this I'll never be able to live with myself, Alice. I'll come back, don't worry. Just keep praying for me."

"You know I will. Just come home."

Buck walked home with those last words running through his head. Just come home. He wanted to ask her to wait for him but didn't feel like he had the right. After all they had only been seeing each other for half a year or so. Somehow he knew that he would always remember that moment when she said those words and gave him a warm kiss. He knew she wanted him to come home. They both wanted to say more but they were sensible and knew that their relationship was new and that they had only been seeing each other a short while. It was nice that there was someone who cared and that was all that was needed for now.

The next few weeks hurried by. Tests were taken, gowns were ordered, yearbooks were signed and friends parted. Graduation came and Buck was surprised when he received the Mathematics award. His family was proud of him and after the ceremony pictures were taken of Buck and his family, Alice and her family and both families together. Buck asked Bobby to take a picture of Alice all by herself, one in cap and gown and the other without the cap and gown. He was anxious to get the pictures back and so they took all the pictures on the roll and brought the film to the drugstore the next morning. The pictures would be ready in a few days.

The Fourth of July was like past holidays. There was a parade down Willis Avenue to Town Hall, a few speeches, and families cooking out. The big problem was getting meat for this special going away party and because they didn't plan far enough in advance, they had to settle for hot dogs. No one really seemed to mind. Alice was over to the Jones's cookout during the afternoon and in the evening Buck and Alice went to the Goodwin's for their party. From their backyard they could see the fireworks that started at nine.

Alice was a pretty young lady and that is what attracted Buck to her when they met in the grocery store. She was about average height with some freckles on her nose and cheeks and blonde hair. And she was smart. Her grades were always good. But they didn't come without effort on her part. She was conscientious and attentive in class and she never missed doing homework. Teachers liked students like Alice.

Buck always liked Mr. Goodwin and he found himself answering questions as to where he wanted to go and what he wanted to do. Buck had to admit that he really hadn't considered where he wanted to fight and what he wanted to do in the service just as long as it helped bring the war to a quicker conclusion. Mr. Goodwin said that it would be wonderful if somehow he could bring freedom to the Philippines as that was the birthplace of Buck's mother and maternal relatives. Buck said that he hadn't considered that but that would make his mother proud if somehow he was instrumental in setting the Philippines free. Mr. Goodwin also suggested that he tell his commanding officer that he was very good at Math. Since not many people were, Mr. Goodwin thought that it might help him get a special assignment.

"Now, don't say anything while you're in boot camp, but if they start testing or ask what skills you have, don't forget to mention that you are a whiz at Math."

"What do you think that will do, Mr. Goodwin?"

"This war is becoming more and more technical and the country that develops and uses that technology will have a big edge when the war is over. I hope you find a spot where your skills and their needs meet. Take if from me, the military doesn't always use their manpower to it's best advantage. Good cooks are made gunners and good gunners are told to be cooks. Try not to let that happen to you, Buck."

"Thanks, Mr. Goodwin. I think that's good advice and I'll remember it. You and Mrs. Goodwin remember me in your prayers, please."

"You know we will."

Alice was watching Buck and her Dad talk. She admired how her boyfriend stood and how respectful he was. She saw his good looks and olive skin which he inherited from his mother and knew that he would be attractive to anyone he met. When Alice saw the men getting ready to part she walked over to them. For the men it seemed like the right time to end their conversation.

"Sounds like you guys had a heavy conversation?"

"I wouldn't say that. Just some good, friendly advice and help. Thanks Mr. Goodwin."

The evening was filled with the impending event that Alice and Buck would soon be separated. And Buck would be in harm's way, if not immediately, eventually. When it was time to say good night and walk home, Buck walked with Alice to the door. When he squeezed her hand it was like a signal that they shouldn't kiss on the steps. They started up the street a bit, where it was a bit darker. Under a maple tree and in semi darkness they kissed, knowing that it might be one of the last times for a while. They still had a few days but this might be the last time that they would be alone. Buck again told Alice that he would return. With a very heavy heart he let go of her hand and walked home.

Sunday the family walked the ten blocks to church and went to eight-thirty Mass. After they came home Mickey asked Buck if he wanted to walk around the school and he said that he did. Mickey wasn't much when it came to sentimental stuff but she knew that she was going to miss Buck's quiet presence. Just his being in the house made home more pleasant. He was a peace maker and somehow managed to negotiate peace between herself and Bobby when they would squabble. Because he was in the house Mom and Dad treated all the kids like they were more grownup than they actually were. Buck was going to be missed.

"Buck, I'm gonna miss you."

"I'll miss you too, Mick."

"What I'm trying to say is that I'll really miss you."

"I know, Mickey. Sometimes it's hard to tell someone what you actually feel. I know that from talking to Alice. I want to tell her so much but it just doesn't come out right. But I will miss you. You are my sister and I love you. There. I wish I could have said that to Alice but I couldn't. But I can say it to you and I do love you. I'll keep your picture near me and when I write to Mom and Dad, know that I'm writing to you in that same letter."

"Thanks, Buck, for saying that. I love you, too, and will write to you while your gone. And I'll pray for you every night without fail."

They walked around the school, through the playground area, the ball fields and well kept grounds where both had spent their grammar school years. Both had many memories of learning to swing on swings, slide on slides, play games and roller skate. Each had the same yet different experiences. Each, however, had pleasant memories. They returned home in time for lunch.

The radio was playing when they reached the house as it often did on days when everyone was home. The song playing was "The White

Cliffs of Dover." He listened to the words, "There'll be bluebirds over, the white cliffs of Dover, tomorrow, just you wait and see. There'll be love and laughter and peace ever after, tomorrow when the world is free." How Buck wanted to believe those words but even with all his naiveté he knew that was asking for too much. Yet the words would go round and round in his head and he just couldn't forget them.

After lunch Buck went over to Alice's and they took a long walk, ending up at the Double Dip Ice Cream Shoppe. Both splurged with a banana split and walked some more just to work off the extra calories. By the time they had returned to her house they had said all there was to say and Buck explained that he would be getting the train at the Williston Park Station at 7:12 in the morning. Bobby would probably walk him there since he had some luggage. He didn't know if Mickey would come or not. Alice said that since the station was such a public place she would give Buck his going away kiss now. And she did. They embraced and Alice whispered that she would write each week. He said that the letters should start after boot-camp and he would be home for a week after that initiation was over. I'll see you then and we'll start writing after that. Tears were in Alice's eyes as she said good night and they separated. Buck walked home slowly in time for a nice supper of pork chops, string beans and potatoes.

The last hours of being with one's family are especially difficult if there is genuine feeling for each other. This family was genuinely concerned for each other and everyone loved Buck. The last hours were a bit awkward. It was agreed that Bobby would walk Buck to the railroad station. Mickey insisted that she wanted to go, too. Bobby said that he would wake her up and if she wanted to go she could or if she wanted to sleep she could do that, too. She knew what she would do.

Lena waited for the right moment and found it when Buck was in the kitchen.

"Buck, I want to say something to you."

"Mom, I know you're going to miss me. I'll miss you, too."

"Yes, but that's not it. I'm going to tell you that I'm proud of what you are doing and I know something that no one else knows. You will come home from this war, unhurt."

"Mom, I know that I'll be OK but I can't promise anything more."

"I'm telling you that you will survive. Remember that when things get rough. Use your smarts and you will survive and make your mother proud."

"What are you telling me, Mom?"

"I'm telling you that you will come home safe, if you keep your head and use your brains. Just remember that," his mother said emphatically and with a bit of annoyance in her voice.

Buck thought this conversation a bit weird. Mom had a premonition but that didn't necessarily make it true. Yet he didn't think he should tell her that he didn't believe her. Now was not the time to argue or disagree. The advice his Mother gave him, however, might be helpful some day. So he sort of humored his Mother by saying that he would think positive and he would keep his wits about him and not do anything stupid and that he knew he would come home safe and sound.

Buck was sitting in the living room when his Father sat down next to him.

"Can you handle some advice about basic training?"

"Sure. I really don't know what to expect."

"It's no mystery but there are a few things you need to know."

"I'm anxious to know, Dad," said Buck.

"A large part of basic is physical. You'll do fine with that because you're a good athlete. It's the mental part that can be tough. They yell at you, speak disrespectfully to you, call you by feminine names and try to get under your skin. They also try to find out who the hotshots are. They give you opportunities to show off and will use that knowledge against you. If you show off too much they'll make you show off for the entire camp. You don't want that. Stay with the group, don't get too far ahead and don't get far behind. Try not to be noticed. Always be respectful and keep away from the tough guys who want to roll dice, play cards and seem to have a chip on their shoulder. You'll recognize them first by their language. They can get you in a lot of trouble."

"Are you telling me not to do my best?"

"No, just do your best but don't show off. Be good but make sure that others are better than you. You know what you can do. Always make it look like your giving one hundred percent even if you only have to give ninety. You'll see what I mean when you get to camp. Stay with the crowd, do well, but don't show off and you'll be fine."

"Dad, I think I know what you mean. I've always given my best in track and in baseball and it may be hard to hold back just a bit. But I'll try it out and see how it works. I'll let you know when I return in six weeks."

Shortly after this discussion they went to bed and Sonny had trouble digesting the practical advice his father gave him and the strange advice his mother gave him. It took him a lot longer to get to sleep than usual but eventually he stopped thinking and sleep overtook him.

Chapter 4

The train ride to Pennsylvania Station in New York City was only forty minutes long with no change of trains. Buck looked out the window as the scenery flew by and he saw houses and trees flash by through the smoke from the engine streaming along behind and along side the train. He thought of the walk to the station. True to her word Mickey got up and walked with Bobby and Buck. Not much needed to be said, only that he would be home in six weeks. He told Bobby that it would be a tough six weeks but he was sure that he would do well. He was in great shape and a good athlete and that should count for something. He told Mickey to keep an eye on Mom and don't let her worry too much. She said that she would.

Once they got to the city Buck found his way to the main lobby and saw a sign that read, "Marine Corps Training Camp." His luggage consisted of a small athletic bag with his personal items like toothpaste, shaving stuff, something to read, a pair of tennis shoes and socks. He was told that they would provide all his clothing. He wondered why so many of the other recruits had so much luggage. At least their bags were much larger than his.

A soldier with three stripes on his arm introduced himself as Sergeant Birdwell. He told Buck to meet some of the other recruits as they had a half hour before they would board the train. He introduced himself to a red headed slim guy by the name of James O'Brien from Boston. They talked about the Boston Red Socks and the Yankees. Buck had to tell him that he didn't really like the Yankees but was a Brooklyn Dodger fan and paid little attention to the Yankees. That made O'Brien feel better. They passed the time talking sports and about school. He had just graduated a week ago, also.

They walked together, about twenty of them, to the train and had an entire car to themselves. He sat with O'Brien as he was very pleasant and some of the others were loud and boisterous. An hour later the train stopped in Philadelphia and another thirty or so recruits boarded. In Washington another fifteen got on before they continued on to Jacksonville, North Carolina. A box lunch was provided shortly after one in the afternoon. At Jacksonville, the recruits got off, but no other passengers embarked. The train was barely away from the station when another Sergeant took charge.

"Recruits, fall in. Get your sorry asses in a straight line. Now!" was his first command.

"Left face. Left not right, hay seed. What a sorry bunch of recruits they sent us this time," he bellowed.

The commands were shouted at them with a set of derogatory remarks accompanying each one, every time. Buck quickly recognized that the sergeant had this routine down as neatly as any comic on a vaudeville stage. But not for a moment would he let on that he wasn't intimidated. From platform to bus and finally to the camp the orders were given and most were experiencing cultural shock. From the loving arms of one's family to the hostile commands of a drill sergeant, these orders were intended to instill fear. For most they had the desired effect.

Hair was cut so that all the new recruits were entirely bald. Everyone went from barber to the showers and any concern for modesty was ignored. Once dry they lined up for clothes, skivvies, as underwear was called, pants, undershirts, dress shirts, shoes and socks. Loaded with all of their clothes they returned to their bunks and got dressed. It amazed Buck that every article of clothing fit him perfectly as did the clothing for his tent mates.

First thing in the morning they were lined up on the drill field doing calisthenics. Buck saw this as a good thing since the better shape he was in the easier it would be to get through boot camp. Then came testing on the obstacle course. He was doing great but allowed himself to fall off the ladder on the hand over hand part of the course. He had to redo that portion of the course. Buck didn't want to be the best at anything. He was told what would happen to him if he was among the top performers. With recognition came increased attention from the drill sergeants and increased expectations. His Dad told him that. He saw James O'Brien doing very well on the obstacle course and made a note of the fact that he probably would be given added attention. Before the day was over he was asked to do fifty pushups and a drill sergeant stood over him pushing him to do them faster. Dad's advice was starting to pay off.

Rifle practice was a part of every day. Buck did well on his first day but felt that he had a long way to go. James really did well. He told Buck that he and his father often went squirrel hunting when he was younger. Gradually Buck learned to keep the rifle steady and to squeeze off the shot. He found, with practice, that he could increase his speed and still squeeze the trigger without jerking the rifle.

He had a bit of trouble with the machine guns. He was around the target but not near as good as James who seemed to be a natural. He stayed with it, however, and knew that in a pinch he could operate a machine gun well enough. It just wasn't his weapon of choice.

The first twenty mile hike took place on a hot day. It started out hot and by noon the temperature was well into the nineties. The first ten miles the recruits marched in formation. Then they let the recruits move at their own pace. Buck walked next to James and they moved at a fairly good pace. About five others were moving faster than they were and James wanted to keep up with them. It was time for Buck to clue James in to what was about to happen.

"James, you don't want to be up there with those other five."

"Why not? We're as good as they are, maybe even better."

"I know that. But all you're doing is calling attention to yourself and that's not smart. They'll have you doing pushups like they did when you did well on the obstacle course."

"Is that what they were doing? I thought I should give it my best."

"If you do," Buck said, "They'll reward you with extra chores, extra exercises, longer hikes and shorter breaks and they'll try harder to break you. Make it look like you're giving it your all then back off about ten percent. If they think your not trying they'll really get on your case. On the obstacle course I purposely let my hands slip on the hand over hand and had to do it over. That reduced my score but they still thought I was giving it everything I had."

They watched the five in the front lengthen their lead and saw that one of the soldiers couldn't keep that pace. He was slowly being drawn back to the pack. That was telling the drill sergeant something and he was glad that he was not that recruit. The miles clicked by and Buck and James were able to keep their pace and at the eighteenth mile they were starting to close up to the front four. Buck hoped that the lead group would be able to keep a decent pace so that they would not catch them. Both James and Buck knew that if they wanted to they could lead the hike. But they didn't want to. And that was smart.

Tired but not exhausted they completed the race in the second pack while those who came in the front pack looked exhausted. The heat had a lot to do with that, as well as the pace that they were trying to keep. Everyone would sleep tonight.

By the end of the first week the recruits were adjusting to addressing their instructors with, "Sir, yes, sir." As the result fewer pushups were being performed. The calisthenics were helping get everyone in shape, limber and strong and the recruits didn't seem as confused as they did the first week. When it came time for another twenty mile hike everyone thought they were ready. What they weren't ready for was to carry a twenty pound knapsack. The four winners of the last hike had special knapsacks given them. Everyone knew that these special knapsacks were heavier. James gave Buck a knowing glance when he got a chance.

This time there was a large group of recruits in the first pack and James and Buck were part of that group. As long as everyone stayed together they would all be fine. It was a blessing that the day wasn't as hot as the previous hike and with some clouds the sun didn't do as much damage. It amazed Buck that the drill sergeants hiked along with the recruits even though they didn't carry knapsacks.

"Why do they keep testing us like this?" asked O'Brien. "Surely they know by now who is going to make it and who isn't?"

"Maybe they do but probably they only know who obviously won't make it. Some guys can fake it for a long time before they crack. Those who are physically incapable will be asked to leave first, then those with emotional problems will start to feel the stress. When we get in combat we'll find out what real stress is and we'll think boot camp was a picnic."

"There are some guys who are having trouble keeping up with most of us. I guess they'll not make it."

"They'll be asked to leave and most already know that they are not ready to be marines. They'll go home, rest a bit and enlist or be drafted into the army. These next couple of weeks are going to be interesting as more and more of us feel the stress. Just hang in there, James. Don't try to make a big show of yourself. Maybe the last week or so we can impress the drill instructors. But not now."

"Jones, your advice has been good, so far. I guess I'll stay with it," O'Brien laughed.

"It's more my father's advice than mine but it made sense to me when he gave it to me and it seems to be working."

"Tell your father that I said thanks."

They marched on in silence. Buck reflected on the fact that he all but lost his first name when he came to the camp. Everyone addressed him as Jones. He didn't mind and was getting used to it. James would call him Buck, sometimes, when they were alone. The only exception to being called Jones was when his name was called, "Jones, M," at mail call. He was not unused to being called by his last name only, like on the baseball team or track team but back in class he was Martin and at home he was Buck. Now he was Jones, day in and day out.

Basic training was hell but with the right attitude and an understanding of what was going on the two friends survived the weeks. Just having someone with whom to talk was helpful and if that person was smart and understanding and sympathetic, that was even better. James O'Brien was all of those things and since physical fitness was at the heart of boot camp, the two survived because they were physically fit. They still had to learn how to make a bed the marine way and what was required for inspection. Rising at four in the morning was never easy. But they did these things routinely and the days turned into weeks. They soon found themselves in the last week of boot camp.

Buck was called into the Captain Leonard's office one afternoon, just before evening mess.

"Jones, I've been going over your file," said Captain Mark Leonard, "and I see that you're good at Math. At least that's what your high school records say. Is that true?"

"Sir, yes, Sir. I like Math and received the Mathematics Achievement Award from Mineola High School."

"Jones, they're looking for recruits that have a Math background for work in radar. This might be right up your alley. Interested?"

"Sir, yes, Sir."

"At ease, Jones. After boot camp you guys get a week off to visit family. Then you would fly to Camp Pendleton in San Diego, California. They would teach you how to operate radar and how to repair them. They didn't tell me what assignment they have in mind but I know they are installing radar in the PBY Catalina for patrol duty. That's one possible assignment."

"I'm interested, Sir."

"Good. I'll let them know that you are willing and capable. Then they'll cut orders for wherever it is they want to send you. I'll tell them you're a good candidate."

"Sir, Thank you, Sir." Then on a more personal tone, "I appreciate you taking a personal interest."

"Jones, every man is important in this war and when you have special skills it would be a mistake not to use them. I hope the assignment turns out to be a good one. Dismissed."

Buck saluted smartly, did an about face and left the captain's office. He was thinking that everything was working out like it should. He would like to learn radar and knew that it would be something he would enjoy. For now, until he heard more news, he would keep this information to himself.

On the last full day of training before everyone was dismissed, Colonel Harold Hess addressed the men. He told them that they just went through basic training and while it was tough it would be nothing compared to what some of them would experience in the next years. He told them that he had to send home a good number because they could not make the grade and weren't fit to be called a marine. Those who did pass basic training were being promoted to Private First Class and would receive stripes to be sewed on by their mothers or girl friends. They would also receive their orders for their assignment as soon as they were dismissed. The assignments would begin as soon as they returned from a short visit home. He also said that he was proud of this class of recruits and held them in high esteem. He encouraged them to uphold the proud traditions of the marines and he felt certain that they would make him, their families and the country proud.

Buck appreciated the sincerity with which the speech was given. Since it was the only encouraging and positive message the men had heard in six weeks, it was noteworthy. They would remember this short ceremony and especially the concept that some would experience very tough times in the years ahead. That was meaningful to Buck.

Buck picked up his stripes and assignment. It was as the Captain had told him. After home leave he would meet in Pennsylvania Station again, be driven by bus to Fort Dix, New Jersey, fly to San Diego and would report for training in radar school at Fort Pendleton, California. He was ready to go home, couldn't wait to see Alice, his parents and brother and sister. First thing in the morning the bus would take them to the railroad station.

James O'Brien was assigned to a base in Florida. The orders stated that he would be trained as a gunner. He was excited about that and he and Buck talked about their paths crossing, maybe sometime in the future. Buck was sorry that he wasn't going to the same camp as James, but knew that he had to do what was best for himself and for the best use of his talents. Both men expressed their appreciation for the support that each gave during basic training. In the morning a sincere handshake had to say what they were unable to put into words.

Chapter 5

Martin Jones met Buck at the Williston Park station with his unmarked police car. It was late in the afternoon when the train arrived, filled with commuters from the city. Martin was waiting on the platform for his son and they found each other easily. Buck and Martin hugged and Martin stepped back to admire his son. He sure looked handsome in his marine uniform and he was brown and trim after six weeks of intensive exercise. As they walked to the car Buck told his father how much he appreciated the advice he had passed on to him. He told him about James O'Brien and how eager he was to impress the drill sergeants. His dad asked if he was able to keep him restrained and Buck told him that once he saw how the hotshots were treated, having to carry extra weight in their knapsacks and doing extra pushups, he understood that it didn't pay to call too much attention to himself.

They pulled into the driveway at 23 Henry Street and Mickey and Bobby came out of the house. Bobby shook hands and grabbed Buck's duffle bag and Mickey hugged him. Then she stepped back and told him that there wasn't a girl in Williston Park who would be able to resist him. Buck colored a bit. Then he saw his mother at the front door and went to hug his Mom.

"You look great, Martin. How did you do in basic training?"

"Mom, I have a lot to tell you. But I must confess that I'm hungry and I've been thinking about your cooking. What's for supper?"

"We can't feed you like they do in the service," said his dad. "Don't you know there's a war on?" He chucked to himself at his little joke.

"I did get some roast beef and with potatoes, gravy, carrots and peas I think we'll have a good meal," said Lena. "Oh, by the way, I invited Alice over for supper. She should be here soon."

Alice arrived and gave Buck a sisterly hug and a not so sisterly kiss. He didn't mind and everyone kept their wise remarks to themselves. They had a tasty supper, lively conversation with Buck the center of attention and genuine pride that he did so well in boot camp. All in all it was a nice evening. At ten o'clock Alice said that it was time for her to go home and Buck walked her home.

"Alice, what are you doing now that you've graduated?"

"I've been filling in at the flower shop since vacation and usually work about four days each week. It's a job and they treat me nice there. The customers are also very nice but the pay isn't so good."

"Are you thinking of something else?" Buck asked.

"I'm still considering college but for now I think I'll get a job at the Sperry Gyroscope Plant in New Hyde Park. A neighbor works there and she said that they're hiring. I'd like to do something that will help the war effort and the pay is good," she said.

"Tell me how that goes. No matter where you work you'll do well."

He stopped in and spoke with the Goodwins for a few minutes, and promised that he would stay longer the next time. He thanked Mr. Goodwin for the advice about trying to get into a technical field and he felt that he would be using his Math skills in the future at radar school. Alice walked him to the door. They stepped outside and she gave him a kiss he would remember. No words were spoken nor were they needed.

The week had passed like he expected. He was treated like royalty and shown off to the neighbors in his dress blue uniform. He answered the same questions over and over and treated each question like it was the first time someone asked it. He enjoyed all the attention but was beginning to tire of being on display. It was soon Monday morning, August 24th and his Dad drove him to the train station. Bobby came along and carried the duffle bag which was fairly heavy and clumsy. He was glad he didn't have to walk to the station. This time saying goodbye was a bit more difficult since Buck didn't know how long he would be in California and when he would ship out. He promised everyone that he would write and his Mom put a writing pad and ten stamped envelopes in his duffle bag to make sure that he did. As he looked out the window from the train he felt that it might be a long time before he returned.

When he arrived at Penn Station he found a group of marines all in dress uniform, all headed for Fort Dix and then California. He met one who was going be a radio man and another who was being trained in navigation. None had ever seen combat before. He recognized a few from basic training. They boarded a bus in front of the huge terminal, drove to Fort Dix and after having their orders checked and verified, they boarded the prop jet for California. Buck managed to get a short nap on the plane as he knew it would be a long day. California was three hours behind New York time. By sundown they arrived at Camp Pendleton, were assigned a bunk in one of the many tents in use, ate supper and were ready to sleep.

A sergeant came to his tent in the morning and called him by the name of Martin Jones. He hesitated a moment, not expecting to hear his full name used. He walked with the sergeant to the mess tent, got a tin of eggs, sausage, some toast and coffee and sat down with him. He was introduced to two other privates, Robert McMurray and Stephen Jablonski. The sergeant introduced himself as Staff Sergeant Charles Levitz. They all ate together. The sergeant said that he would show them around and at ten hundred hours they were to report to the radar training facility. Breakfast took about ten minutes and they left for a tour of the camp. Buck was anxious to start radar training. In the long run it would save a lot of time if he knew where everything was. Sergeant Levitz seemed to know that.

At ten hundred hours they were delivered to a Captain Brewster who showed them to a classroom. When they were all present he told them that they would be taking a test. Buck wanted to say that he didn't have time to prepare but thought better of it. He was glad that he didn't say anything since he didn't find the test difficult. It was a good test of a person's basic knowledge of Mathematics. That afternoon he met in a class with fifteen other new recruits who were being introduced to the world of radar. McMurray and Jablonski were included. He was glad that he was comfortable with Math as he began to understand why that knowledge would be essential to learning how radar worked.

The training was intense but interesting. His fellow students seemed sharp, asked astute questions and were serious about the training. It moved along fairly well but there was a lot to memorize. Learning and understanding came easy but doing and operating the equipment was awkward and clumsy. By the end of the first week, Buck was proud of all that he had learned. The training went on every day for four weeks with the exception of Sunday. They did quit at fifteen hundred hours each Saturday afternoon. On Saturday, September 19th Captain Brewster announced that this entire class would be sent to Kaneohe Bay. He told the class that new radars were being installed in PBY Catalinas, as the patrol planes were called, and they would be taught how to install and repair the new radar. One student asked the question that all wanted to ask.

"Sir, where is Kaneohe Bay?"

"You'll be pleased to hear that it is in Hawaii, on the island of Oahu, just over the mountains from Honolulu," responded Captain Brewster.

The entire class spontaneously clapped.

"When do we leave?" was the next question.

"Monday, September 21st. Make your phone calls home tonight and tomorrow. You can tell them you're going to Hawaii but that's it. You'll be there several weeks while your PBY is being outfitted with the new radar and you become familiar with them. You also have to learn all there is to know about handling yourself in a PBY. Emergency procedures, all the equipment and procedures will have to be mastered. You'll most likely go on a few trial runs. You may not get a chance to speak with your family after you get there so tell them that you will correspond by letter after you leave here. The Navy will censor all letters so that you don't give away any information as to troop movements and what we're planning. We are up against a very cunning enemy."

After a brief pause he asked, "Any other questions?"

Since no one had any questions the Captain was about to dismiss the men. Then he added that he heard a bit of scuttlebutt and thought the men in front of him would like to hear what he heard. He said that starting in October the government was going to lower the draft age to eighteen. He told the men that he wasn't positive but his source was usually accurate and since they would be leaving for Hawaii on Monday they would probably like to hear the rumor. He told the men that he was certain they would be thankful that they enlisted when they did.

That evening Buck phoned his family and then made a call to Alice. He told her that he would be going to a base in Hawaii and would get familiar with the radar that was being installed. He said that he probably would be going on some training missions but didn't think that they would involve action. He promised that he would write but that a censor would read every letter and he would have to be careful with how much he could say. She told him that she would pray for him and she wished him every success. He said that he carried her picture around in his wallet and he appreciated that she was praying for him. They painfully said goodnight and hung up the receivers.

Chapter 6

Sitting in a jump seat in a cargo plane was not comfortable and there were no windows to brighten up the interior. They were told there was nothing to see except ocean and they would see plenty of that in the weeks ahead. So the men relaxed and tried to get some sleep. The plane touched down at Kaneohe Bay on an airfield that looked like it had taken several direct hits, judging by the repairs. This was the first place to experience the wrath of the Japanese before they continued on to Pearl Harbor just over the mountains.

As they stepped off the plane they felt the warm ocean breeze blowing across their faces. They could see mountains in the distance and water on about three sides. If one had to choose a place for training, this would be as good a choice as any. A bus picked the men up and drove them to their barracks about a half mile from the hangers. Buck figured it to be less than a ten minute walk. They got supper in the mess hall and had a few minutes to walk around the base. How clean and lush everything looked. He could see the ocean and spray from waves that crashed against the volcanic rocks. In the other direction he saw the beautiful blue green mountains. Buck knew that this was where this ugly war started and that there was nothing pretty about war, except maybe the scenery. That he was taught to appreciate.

The next morning they were delivered to the airfield and got a tour of their new home away from home. The PBY Catalina sat on the edge of the runway, black and huge. It was designated VPB-13. They had the opportunity to walk around it, inspecting it from every angle and having the chance to ask questions. When they completed the outside they climbed into the patrol plane for a tour of the interior. Their Captain, Ralph Taylor, was a tall lanky pilot from Nashville, Tennessee and he gave the crew the tour. Buck immediately saw where the radar was installed, behind the navigator, just behind the cockpit. The other four crewmen were gunners and would take positions at the two waist "blister" windows, the forward nose position and in the lower slot below the tail. Rudy Koch, a wiry boy from Cleveland was to occupy the forward gunnery position in the nose and Ricky Graves, also small and wiry, was assigned the position below the tail in what the men called, "the tunnel." The other two gunners were assigned the waist blister positions.

That first morning the men found that the plane had a cruising speed of 117 knots per hour and a maximum speed of 179 knots per hour, at least on paper. They also found that seldom would the plane reach 100 knots and more likely it would seldom achieve 90 knots per hour. Before Captain Taylor could get out the rest of the information, questions were being directed at him.

"How high can this thing fly?"

"What's the range of this plane?"

"Hold on, hold on. I'm getting to all of that. The plane can fly at a ceiling of 13,000 feet. It has a range of 2,350 miles, conditions being favorable. Koch, you'll have two .30-caliber machine guns in the bow position, and Graves, you'll have a .30-caliber in the rear ventral hatch. Meyer and Thompson, you'll each have a .50-caliber gun in the waist blister positions. I don't care who will be in which position. You guys decide."

Reggie Meyer was a skinny, tall blond from Los Angeles. He was fast with a joke and was very clever with his remarks. He wasn't mean and meant no harm even though his wit could be a bit barbed, at times. Neal Thompson was from Portland, Oregon and was the strong silent type. He had a scar on his lip which he said came from playing with his brother when he got cut with a boy scout knife. Those were the gunners and all understood that each one would learn how to fire both guns. Probably no one would be taking Rudy's place in the bow position since it was a very tight fit and several of the men were just too big. Possibly Ricky would be able to fit into the forward position but most likely nobody else. Rudy claimed that he had the best view and no one doubted that he was correct.

Captain Taylor said that they would be taking "the cat," as the Catalina was called, up for a brief flight around the island so that the men would get a feel for the plane. There was still a lot to learn before they were ready for combat. Buck took his seat where the radar console would be installed.

He would be involved in the installation in some way. As of that moment he didn't know how.

The co-pilot was First Lieutenant Paul Dwyer. He came from a suburb of Chicago and was very pleasant to be around. Like the captain he was a commercial pilot before joining the marines and was thirty-two years old. The Captain was the old man at thirty-five. The rest of us were just kids out of high school although Reggie Meyer had a year of college and was twenty.

Steve Winters was the navigator and had learned what he needed to know from the marines. He seemed to be a natural, was always interested in Geography, Math and Science and just loved plotting the best routes between places, taking into account distance, wind and weather. To him it was a game and he enjoyed his work. He said that he had a highly developed sense of direction and was interested in the stars from childhood. That could be helpful if they ever lost their compass.

The bombardier was Joe Schmidt. He told everyone that he was fine with being called Schmidt or Schmitty but not Smith or Smitty. Most called him Joe or Schmidt. He was from Milwaukee where his father worked in a beer factory. He told the marines that he wanted to drop bombs on the Japanese, so they sent him for training as a bombardier and he did very well, coming out in the top 10% of his class. He was anxious to learn all there was to know about this "black cat" the nickname for the Catalina.

That afternoon they got a tour of the islands from the PBY. Two men could stand at each waist blister and view the beautiful volcanic islands below. Rudy climbed into his forward position and Ricky tried to get comfortable in his. The men took turns at the various positions and got a chance to check out the galley and the living quarters. They learned that the PBY could land on the sea as well as on land. Since the flying boat could stay up almost twenty-four hours they would be taking turns in the hammocks, getting some sleep when they could. They began to understand how valuable this plane-boat could be for rescue since they could land on the water. The PBY would be invaluable for patrol duty, especially in finding submarines when the subs would come up for air and recharging in the early evening. Schmidt said that he looked forward to dropping several bombs down the cunning tower of a sub or the smokestack of a freighter.

The afternoon was almost over when they returned to the airfield. They met with some technicians and Buck was told that his services would be required when they installed the radar in about an hour. He decided to get a bite to eat in case the installation took all evening. He returned to the plane before the technicians arrived but barely had time to look around before the truck with the equipment arrived.

As they were installing the radar one of the technicians gave Buck a running account of what was being done. He told him where he was most likely to experience difficulties and showed him how to make the necessary connections should power be lost. The technician told him the range of the radar but also told Buck to do his own calculations so that he would understand the size and intensity of each blip. He explained that this radar, the AN/APS-2 could detect ships at a distance of about 60 miles depending on the size of the ship. Aircraft, depending on size would be a lot less. He suggested that Buck test out the radar on known American aircraft to get an idea of the distance that each could be perceived and what kind of a pattern each would show on the radar screen. Buck knew that he had his work cut out for him for the next weeks. He learned that he would be expected to fix his own radar if things went wrong and was told that he would have no trouble as they were trouble free except for when they needed to be replaced. He was told that due to the erratic nature of the electricity in the plane, a fuse would blow from time to time and he learned where and how big a fuse would be needed. He felt confident that he would be able to handle any problems.

The next days were spent practicing drills in case of emergency. If there was a fire, where were the extinguishers kept and how to turn on the carbon dioxide controls to put out flames that could ignite the fuel. Should the plane lose altitude, who would get the rafts and what needed to be done to prepare for landing on the sea. The men practiced many different scenarios and soon found that they were increasing their speed, avoiding each other in tight quarters and becoming confident that they knew what they were doing. Then they switched tasks so that everyone would be familiar with the other person's job. The captain impressed on them that while this was practice, there would be a very good chance that these lessons would be used sometime in the course of the war. You could never be too prepared.

Each day they would get in some flying time. Buck got the opportunity to locate ships on his radar screen and to check their size and speed. He felt that he had a good feel for ships but was not as secure with aircraft. So he concentrated on aircraft. Captain Taylor would ask Buck what kind of a plane he was looking at on his screen and Buck would guess at what it might be, its location and approximate speed. Once it could be seen they would tell Buck what it actually was and he would make note of it. Gradually his guesses improved and the Captain told him that he was definitely improving in his recognition.

One day they made some bombing runs on ships that were waiting to be sunk. Joe had been patient while Buck was learning all about radar and was getting anxious about practicing his skills. He was pleased to finally get some action. The runs were made at low, medium and high altitudes so that Joe could get a good feel for his new instrument. He was using ordinance that exploded when it hit but didn't do much damage. This gave Joe a good idea of how well he was doing. And like Buck, he got better with practice. Every chance he got, Joe asked the Captain to make a bombing run. He asked Ricky to give him a report from his position on each bomb that was dropped. He wanted to know how near or far from the target it was. Then Joe kept his own score.

In the barracks that night, Captain Taylor came in and told them that "the cat" was being armed and they would be going on a real mission in the morning. Three cats would be going and they would have an escort at least part of the time. This flight would most likely be for about twenty hours. He told his men to get a good night's sleep as tomorrow would be a long day.

The following morning the three crews were briefed on their assignment. They would be searching for several flyers who were believed shot down. They were headed in the general direction of Johnson Atoll, that is southwest of Oahu. At dusk they would be searching for Japanese submarines on the surface for recharging. No American ships were on their flight path so they could feel confident that any ships spotted would be the enemy. This was their first patrol and it was Thursday, October 1st. Buck was excited and anxious for action as were all the men, possibly with the exception of the pilot and co-pilot. It was because they knew what could happen and were feeling the burden of responsibility.

The morning and afternoon were filled with looking and searching the sea with binoculars. The radar blips stopped after they were about an hour from Oahu, once the local air and sea traffic was left behind. The three planes flew at the same speed and altitude but separated by a fair distance. Radios were tested the first hour. Then silence was the order of the day. By late afternoon even the pilot was hoping for some action. No life raft was spotted. Buck took a short breather and got a cup of coffee as the sun was nearing the horizon. He hoped that with the dusk and darkness they would find a submarine. But that didn't happen. About nine in the evening the three planes turned around and started back to Hawaii. They remained on alert until they were almost home. Everyone performed well. The crew got along with no problems but were disappointed that they were unable to find anything. The captain assured them that even the fact that they found nothing was information that naval intelligence would find useful.

They rested the next day and flew out the following day, leaving around noon. This time they went west and they flew by themselves toward Wake Island. It was about eight when Buck got a blip on the radar.

"Captain, I've got a bogey at two o'clock. It's on the surface and it's small."

"We'll go down. Battle stations everyone. Buck, keep an eye out for any escorts."

"Aye, aye, Sir."

It was all business now. Schmidt was ready in the bombardier's bay and bombs were being readied to be dropped.

"Captain, he's moving."

"Let's go in. Are we on target?"

"We're going right down his wake. But the blip is smaller. Now it's gone."

"Schmidt, drop two bombs when I give the signal."

"Right. I'm ready."

"Drop them."

The bombs were dropped at a black sea and they exploded on impact but with little hope of any success. The plane crisscrossed the area several times but no more blips appeared. The crew was a bit dejected when the plane headed back home.

"That's OK men. We've disrupted their evening and it may be a while before he resurfaces. I think he heard us before we were within range.

"What can we do, Captain, so that he won't hear us. How can we sneak up on him?" Buck asked.

"No one has an answer for us yet on that one," said the Captain.

The navigator, Steve Winters, who enjoyed figuring wind and distance said that the enemy had the wind at their back and would have heard the PBY from several miles more than was normal. He suggested that they give any bogeys a wide birth and attack like a hunter from down wind.

"How much more time would that give us, Steve?"

"It all depends on the wind and the humidity. If we're flying into a stiff headwind we'll practically be on top of them before they hear us. They might see us but they'll have a more difficult time hearing us."

"That's sure worth a try. Let's keep that in mind for our next bogey."

The night ended and the morning began as the plane was returning to their airfield. Rather than being down they felt that they might have hit on a technique that would help them bag a few subs. It sure was worth the try. The first rays of light were rising over the mountains as the crew stowed their gear and headed for breakfast and a few hours of sleep.

Chapter 7

The men of VPB-13 were assigned to Noumea on New Caledonia on the edge of the Coral Sea. It was a long flight but they did patrol duty along the way and stopped for fueling twice. A PBY is capable of landing on the ocean, providing it isn't too rough, and getting fueled from a tanker. This could greatly extend the range of a patrol. They didn't do it much because the PBY could stay in the air for almost a day, making refueling unnecessary. But it was possible.

When they landed in Noumea they noticed the humidity and heat immediately. They were in the tropics and south of the equator where it was spring. They went on patrols the first week they were on the island and on a return trip to base they were told by radio of a flyer who needed to be rescued. They were given his last coordinates and before the sun set they saw the yellow raft bouncing in the ocean. The PBY landed nearby and taxied over to the raft. The pilot was thrilled to be picked up so soon and thanked the crew profusely. It pleased the crew to know that they did something very important. They participated in their first rescue.

After several weeks they were asked to fly to Espiritu Santo, an island about eight hours north of Noumea. It was to be their new home base. The men spoke of finally getting some action. They knew that Guadalcanal was several hours away by air and there was plenty of action there. When Steve got his new maps, he and Buck spent time looking at them. Steve was interested in knowing the prevailing winds so he could accurately plot a course and Buck wanted to know the winds so he could recommend to the captain the best way to attack a target.

In late October the men of VPB-13 went out almost every night. The flights were shorter but much more interesting. They were instructed not to engage warships in battle but to pass on the name, number and size of all ships and convoys that they could see. The gunners were especially busy watching out for air cover. Buck stayed glued to the radar screen.

One evening, moments after the sun went below the horizon, Buck spotted a small blip on his radar.

"Captain, a bogey at 340 degrees. Small, not moving, probably a sub."

"Let's try out our new technique. Steve, what would be the best approach?"

Stay on this course until we get west of him. If we attack between 30 and 40 degrees he'll have a hard time hearing us with all the wind that's up tonight. It's dark enough that he probably won't see this black cat either."

"Let's try it. Battle stations, everyone."

The plane descended to about 100 feet above the ocean and continued on a westerly course giving the sub a wide berth. The blip remained on the edge of the radar screen until Buck told the Captain to come about to a heading of about 30 degrees. They did and Buck asked for another five degrees.

"We're dead on, Captain."

"Great! Joe, I don't know how many bombs you can drop but make sure you drop enough."

Joe replied, "Right, Captain."

Rudy called up from his front position that he could see something dead ahead.

"Rudy, start firing when you're in range."

The plane made its run at the sub and took it completely by surprise. They were probably expecting trouble from the east, not the southwest. When Rudy started to fire, they didn't know whether they should return fire or submerge. They ran to their guns, then abandoned that idea for submerging. Valuable seconds were wasted, however. Rudy was firing both his guns, raking the deck continuously. Joe could see the sub and the Captain was steering the plane right toward its stern. Three of the four bombs hit the sub and within seconds it exploded, still not yet submerged. There was no doubt about this kill. The entire crew let out a yell, the first truly celebratory noise since they were joined together as a crew. Buck cheered with the rest but kept his eyes on the radar. He didn't want to be jumped by any Zeros after having inflicted damage on the enemy. They continued northeast for a short while, resumed cruising altitude and completed their patrol duties. Later when they headed southeast for home, the talk was still lively. This was one emotional crew. There is nothing like success to help men to bond and feel like they are part of the team.

In the next month they made daily flights, mostly patrol and several search and rescue. They rescued two airmen on two consecutive days and the following afternoon they caught a freighter hiding between two islands, probably making repairs. They received some fire from the freighter but Rudy got in some good licks. As the plane turned, the waist blister raked the deck and set the ship ablaze. They made a run at her as sailors were abandoning ship. Joe dropped several bombs right on target. The celebration was much more subdued this time as this was what they were supposed to do and they were doing it superbly. Also, they heard daily of a patrol plane being lost, or several Allied planes being shot down. Everyday more men gave their lives on the island of Guadalcanal or other islands in the Solomon Island chain. This was deadly business and these men were getting good at their job. The need to cheer had passed.

The battle of Guadalcanal continued and every night patrols went out alerting the Americans to the movement of the Japanese. On the evening of October 31st the crew of Captain Ralph Taylor was given a patrol route that was very specific and with instructions not to engage the enemy. If the enemy was spotted they were instructed to get their number and direction and remain unseen if possible. They patrolled all night and returned to base the morning of November 1st. They heard that the Americans had landed on Bougainville and had defeated the Japanese in a naval battle. It was the goal of the Americans to take and destroy Rabaul, a Japanese stronghold and supply base and the key to the entire Solomon-New Guinea campaign. The submarine base on Rabaul allowed the Japanese to refuel and continue their deadly damage to the Allied supply lines. While the men hated to allow Japanese ships to move unmolested, they also knew that patrolling and passing on vital information was more important. Subs and freighters were fair game but when it came to war ships they had more firepower and the PBY was a big slow bird and an easy target, much too valuable as a patrol craft to lose. So they bided their time and continued to patrol and rescue.

On the morning of November 15th, after returning from a night patrol just north of Guadalcanal they were told that they were to have a day off. They were told that they would be on an extended patrol starting on Tuesday, November 17th. The plane would make a landing on the ocean to take on fuel and would then patrol the seas between the Caroline and Marshall Islands. They didn't have a code talker on board so Joe Schmidt was given the code phrases and the frequencies he could use to communicate any information that needed to be relayed. The need to stay out of sight was stressed. The patrol sounded routine except for the rendezvous with an oil tanker and the extended time in the air. While the plane was being serviced the crew would get some needed time off.

Buck caught up on his sleep and listened to Armed Forces Radio as he wrote letters home to his family and Alice. He was so absorbed by the war, his nightly patrols and getting ready for the next patrol that he hardly had time for thinking of home. When he started writing he knew how much he missed them and wanted to be there with them. He tried to tell them that but he felt that maybe he wasn't saying exactly what he felt. In any case he wrote two long letters, careful to not say anything that could help the enemy but filled with information about his life, his crew mates, the scenery and the things he missed. While he wrote he heard the tune, "Bewitched, Bothered and Bewildered." They also played "Chattanooga Choo Choo" and memories of riding the train to boot camp and meeting at Pennsylvania Station in New York seemed so long ago. He prayed that the war would end soon and the dying would stop.

Chapter 8

The day dawned clear and windless. While the wind was quiet at dawn it would most likely not stay that way. The wind had a way of surprising you and by late afternoon the breeze had to be respected. The men met in the briefing room and were told that an operation was underway that did not need any surprises. Most of the usual channels of Japanese troop movements were under surveillance. But the area between the Marshall Islands and Caroline Islands could be a source of trouble if the Japanese were sending ships through that route. Because their patrol mission needed about thirty hours in the air they would be meeting with an oil tanker fairly near the equator about five that afternoon. Steve was given the tanker's course and he was to figure out where on the course they would meet the tanker. Joe was also given the tanker's radio frequency to be used only if necessary.

At the late hour of 0900 hours the PBY lifted off from the island of Espiritu Santo headed north. It flew all day at cruising altitude with nothing showing up on radar but some islands. And even though they were in the tropics, at 13,000 feet it could be cool. Most of the crew wore their flight jackets. When they reached the course that the tanker was taking, they changed direction to a bearing of 30 degrees. Steve estimated that they would be early since they were blessed with a slight tailwind. As it happened the tanker showed up on radar when it was expected.. The "big black cat" could not be mistaken and a flash of lights from the tanker greeted the PBY. They made a smooth landing to the stern of the tanker and taxied up to the ship which was now stopped. It didn't take long to fill up the tanks and to give the Catalina another twenty-two or so hours in the air. Pleasantries were exchanged and the men on the tanker were properly thanked for the service. The co-pilot, Paul Dwyer, headed the plane into the wind and after a fairly long run on the water they were airborne.

The evening was uneventful and the men took turns getting several hours sleep. When Buck took his nap, Joe covered for him and kept his eyes on the screen. Steve alerted him to when an island might be expected. Ralph and Paul, pilot and copilot each took two hours between midnight and before dawn. The gunners could all take time off just about any time as long as several stayed on alert. The coffee was constantly being brewed and was most welcome after waking. Normally they would have been bored with the lack of activity but the men knew that not finding a convoy was a good sign for the forces ready to go into battle.

It was at 0600 hours that the plane did a 90 degree turn and headed west toward the Caroline Islands. An hour later they turned south and headed back toward Espiritu Santo, their home base. Even with stiff winds they could make their base but with tail winds from the northeast they would have plenty of fuel. They were hoping that on the return voyage they would see no convoy steaming toward Bougainville. At mid morning they passed over several small islands in the Carolinas. But no enemy activity was spotted. The morning passed slowly with the men taking turns in the galley and eating K rations, better know as "an airman's lunch." They weren't too great for taste but when you were finished you were no longer hungry. It was shortly after noon that Buck let out a yell.

"Bogey at two o'clock. Above us."

All eyes tried to spot the bogey but clouds were in the way and the sun was bright.

"Take it down, Captain," Buck yelled. "It's most likely a Zero. Let's hope he hasn't seen us."

Captain Taylor made a ninety degree turn to the east and put the PBY into a steep descent. "Battle stations, everyone," was an unnecessary command but executed anyway.

"He saw us. He's coming after us, Captain," Buck told everyone by radio.

"We'll take it as low as we can. Maybe he'll miscalculate and not be able to pull out of his dive and land in the water. Neal, you'll get the first shot at him," said the Captain.

Neal and Reggie were both looking through the same waist blister when Reggie spotted a black spot gaining on them. "He's tough to see coming at us out of the sun."

"This guy must know what he's doing. Fire when he's in range, Neal."

The sound of 0.50-caliber guns going off broke the sound of the plane's descent. Suddenly three or four rounds from the Zero ripped through the fuselage.

"Anyone hurt?" asked Lieutenant Dwyer.

He was greeted by a chorus of "no." Rudy was the only one not easily visible and he called out that he was fine but didn't get a shot off at him as he climbed too fast.

"Buck, tell me if he's making another pass. I think he may have hit our fuel line."

"He's turning, Captain. He'll be coming back out of the sun like he did before."

"Joe, you and Ricky get the life rafts and emergency gear. Ricky, we're so low to the ocean now that he'll never get below us. Prepare for an emergency landing. Make sure everyone has their life jackets on. We're going to keep flying so we're not sitting ducks."

On the second pass the PBY took several rounds in the tail. The captain could feel the change in the way the plane handled and told the crew. Neal said that he thought he might have hit the Zero. So far there was no evidence of a hit.

"Buck, grab that water container and as much of the rations that you can and when the rafts are put in the water, throw them in. Then get in one of the rafts and tie both together. We're going to have to ditch soon. She's not going to stay together much longer."

The two waist gunners stayed with their guns but the rest of the crew prepared for an emergency landing. The plane landed smoothly enough as the seas were relatively calm and the PBY was made for landing on water. The plane came to a very quick stop, although the Captain kept the motor running so he could taxi the plane to give as small a target as possible and allow both waist gunners to get in some shots. The hatch was opened and the two black rafts were inflated and dropped into the sea. The first raft was blown behind the PBY because of the propeller wash. Buck kept a rope in his hand as he jumped into the water to prevent that from happening to the second raft. The PBY was still moving forward and Buck pulled in the second life raft. The scream of the Zero was getting louder when shots from the Zero raked the Catalina. Flames shot up from the wing. Joe Schmidt was hit just as he was getting ready to jump. His body temporarily blocked the exit. Then the plane exploded. Debris was thrown in all directions and there was a tremendous burst of flames. Buck was in the water about fifty feet from the tail of the plane and couldn't believe what had just happened. His plane and crew members were destroyed in an instant and all that remained was some debris on the ocean.

As the Zero climbed there was a small puff of black smoke that trailed from the engine. Buck hoped that this would mean that he would high-tail-it for home and might not make it back to base to brag about his kill. The silence that followed was ominous. After twenty-seven or so hours of hearing a motor there was suddenly only the gentle breezes of the wind and the lapping of the waves against the raft. Buck climbed into the larger of the two rafts, unlashed a paddle and went after the loose raft. He soon retrieved it and tied the two rafts together.

Never in his life did Buck feel so alone. He had just lost his entire family, at least his military family. The men he worked with and depended on and grew to love as brothers disappeared in one mighty explosion. How could this have happened? He would need time to think about all of this and to grieve. For now all he could do was look at the small amount of debris left floating on the water after the plane sunk and say a prayer that God would take his friends to Himself. Soon, except for an oil slick, it was like they never existed. Tears involuntarily rolled down his cheeks, the first time in many years that he cried.

Chapter 9

Lena Jones woke from a sound sleep with a small cry. It was a few minutes past midnight by the clock on the end table.

"Lena, what's the matter?"

"Nothing, Martin, just a dream," she said. "I'm going downstairs for a few minutes. Maybe get a glass of milk."

Martin murmured something and turned over to return to sleep. Lena went downstairs but didn't go to the refrigerator for milk. She went to the front window and looked out. The street was silent. Then she sat down in her rocker, blessed herself and began her prayer. She had a premonition that something had happened. No, it was more than a premonition. She knew that Buck had encountered some danger and she wanted to talk to God about what was happening. She was still for a long time, maybe thirty or forty minutes. When she finally blessed herself and got up she was at peace. She had prayed the "Our Father" and said so many times that "God's will be done." She eventually came to the realization that his will was being done. What more could she ask for? That is what she must accept. She asked herself what day it was. It was November 17th. No, it was after midnight so it was the start of November 18th, a Wednesday. She returned to bed with a deep sense of peace and the belief that her son was alive.

In the morning, Martin was up early as usual and Lena got up with him, which was unusual. She told him of her premonition but assured him that she was certain that Buck had survived and would be safe. Martin didn't know what to make of all of this. He had known Lena for twenty years and knew that she wasn't a religious kook. Deeply spiritual but not a nut job. She was good, loving, a great mother and dedicated to loving

God and helping her neighbor. He suggested that they not tell Bobby and Mickey. If there was bad news they would hear soon enough. He left for work with a vague feeling that maybe Lena was obsessing a little too much about Buck. He would watch for other signs but just this once didn't make a pattern.

When Martin sat down at his desk he was greeted with a lot of information that he asked for the day before but which had not arrived. Here it was, background material that he knew would be useful. He began his day's work. He and another detective left the precinct to ask some questions of a potential witness and the morning's concerns about Lena were forgotten.

Chapter 10

The sea was relatively calm with the wind blowing from the northeast. Buck couldn't tell for a while as the sun was overhead and west could have been anyplace on the compass. So he busied himself finding out what resources he had. The big life raft had water for five men for two days and rations for five for two days also. There was a flashlight and extra batteries, a utility knife with several tools on it, four paddles, a pair of binoculars, a survival kit with matches and a first aid kit. The smaller raft had about the same supplies except it was for four people. There were no binoculars in that raft. Buck kept the two rafts tied together and decided to wait until tomorrow before making a decision as to whether or not to keep both rafts and if not, which one to destroy. He also had to figure out what he would need. As the sun moved in the sky, Buck used the shadow from the paddle to tell him that he was moving southwest. He remembered the maps that Steve was using to navigate and he felt that most of the islands would be to the northwest. Maybe he could aim in that direction. To do that he would need a sail and a rudder.

By the late afternoon Buck's clothes were dry. He had taken off his life vest and tied it to one of the handles on the raft. He didn't want to be without his vest if the seas got rough. His flight jacket might not be needed but he had it anyway. Then he remembered that he had a few rations in the inside pocket. He pulled a ration from his pocket for supper. It looked like a candy bar but was much more nutritious. His thoughts went to considering how he would feed himself even if he found an island. He was glad for the time being that his life rafts were black, making it more difficult for the Japanese to spot him if they were in the area. He didn't think there were too many allied planes and ships in the area. His thoughts increasingly turned to his precarious position and what he would need to do to survive.

As he searched through the pockets and hiding places in the raft he realized that he had many items which might be useful, depending on his situation. He saw flairs and made a special note to remember where they were. He found a sponge and used it to empty some of the water in the bottom of the raft. He found a repair kit, a mirror for signaling and some seasickness tablets. Flairs and the mirror would be essential if he saw a rescue plane or boat. He didn't think he would need the seasickness tablets. The food and water would be essential and he would ration it carefully since he had no idea how long he would be adrift. Even if he found an island he would have to be concerned with how he would find food. He found a fishing kit as he was searching the big raft and knew that he could get used to eating fish daily. He would like a more varied diet but fish would keep him alive. His fears were allayed a bit.

The sun was warm but not as bad as it could be if it wasn't November. Buck was not fair like many and so was not as concerned about a sunburn. Yet he felt that he needed to take precautions with regard to the sun beating down on him in the tropics. For the time being keeping a shirt on would do the trick.

There were four paddles in the big raft. He secured one in a hand hold in the bow and it stayed vertical. Then he put his flight jacket over the paddle and extended the arms. He could feel that the wind was pushing the jacket a bit. He had plenty of extra rope both from the big raft and from the smaller raft. He didn't cut the rope but used it to keep the jacket open as much as possible. This helped a bit. Then he took another paddle and inserted the wide end in the sleeve and the narrow end toward the other sleeve. He did the same thing again and he had an effective sail. At least he would go a little faster, which might be good or bad. With the fourth paddle as a rudder he was able to change the direction of the raft a bit. As he turned north he felt the raft slipping toward the west as well as moving a bit north. The raft worked best if it was on a broad reach with the wind blowing it from behind but if turned so that he would be on a beam reach the raft would move forward and slide sideways at the same time. He would definitely need a keel if he was to try and sail the raft. He settled for going west and slightly north as the wind varied behind him. He was also surprised how quickly he was getting the knack of sailing this little raft. Memories of his boy scout days at Camp Wawepek on Long Island where he learned to sail returned to him. He hoped some of those lessons would help him now. Buck drank some of the precious water and prepared for a long evening. He watched where the sun was going down and got his bearing and determined that he was definitely going west if he did nothing and northwest if he used the rudder. He decided to take down the sail for the evening until he could make up his mind where he wanted to go. As he did so he noticed that the raft slowed a bit, almost imperceptible.

The terrible feeling of loss came over him again as the sky put on a beautiful show. He couldn't believe that in one split moment the PBY blew up with the entire crew, except himself. In his mind he saw and heard each of his brothers and fellow warriors. He began to realize how much he loved each one and how much he would miss them. He felt better but knew it would be a long time before he would recover.

The sun sets quickly in the tropics and Buck experienced that this Wednesday evening. Soon the heavens were filled with stars and Buck quickly found the big and little dipper and Polaris, the north star. By its nearness to the horizon, Buck could tell that he wasn't far above the equator. He was, however, in the northern hemisphere. How alone and small he felt as he looked up and saw the millions of stars.

For now he hoped the weather would remain calm. He felt the need for a place to sleep and so used his flight jacket for a bed. His prayers, as he drifted off turned to his family. "Mom, Dad, Bobby, Mickey, I'm all right. Alice, I'm all right." Then he thought of his fellow crewmates again and he asked God to accept them and to give their families the strength to get through this terrible ordeal. He didn't voice it but he kept thinking, "Why me, God?" With that thought in mind he drifted off to sleep.

Chapter 11

The wind had picked up a bit during the night although it was still blowing from the northeast. Buck was surprised that the sun was already up and warming him before he woke up. "How could he have slept so long in a somewhat uncomfortable position in a moving raft?" He soon remembered what a stressful and disastrous day he had just experienced and figured that maybe shock was involved. He was right about that even if he didn't want to admit it.

With the increase in wind, Buck noticed that it came more from the east than previously. He found the compass in the survival kit and so was able to accurately verify the direction. The compass was on a string and Buck tied the string near the stern of the raft. He could get along without a compass but life was much easier with it. One never knew when it would be essential.

Buck varied the rations and sipped water conservatively. He saw that C, D and K rations were included and knew that he had enough food for the time being and even for quite a few days on the ocean. What he didn't know was how long he would be afloat and when he would find an island. He wondered what it would hold by way of food. He would take one problem at a time and his current problem was to find land.

The flight jacket was repositioned like the day before and with the wind coming from behind he was able to steer the raft almost to northwest on the compass. That was a guess but from what he saw of the map, that would be where he would want to steer. Now all he could do was hope the wind didn't go crazy on him and the seas remained calm and he was headed toward an island.

A second day passed without incident and the sky put on a tremendous display at sunset. The rocking rhythm of the life raft and the darkness made sleep come easy. Buck's last thoughts on this Thursday was that he was so lucky to be alive and he hoped that he would soon be rescued. His backup prayer was that he would soon reach land. With a last look at the magnificent plethora of stars in the night sky he fell asleep.

The morning was calmer than the day before and Buck was awake just as the sun was rising. As if anticipating that he would be right next to an island he stood up and looked around. Then he got the binoculars out of their pocket and searched the horizon. Nothing but ocean. He knew that being right on the water didn't allow him to see too far but with the binoculars he could increase the distance considerably. Nevertheless there was no land in sight.

To keep busy and to prevent himself from getting out of shape he did exercises. Sits ups could be done easily with his legs under the seats. He could also do pushups and all sorts of stretching exercises. As the sun rose higher in the sky, Buck shed some clothes and was soon dressed only in skivvies. He thought about swimming but decided that it might not be safe. For now he didn't consider it safe as he was concerned that there could be sharks. He also considered the possibility that he could get separated from his rafts and that would be a disaster. He would confine his exercise to the raft.

In mid afternoon he again searched the horizon with binoculars. He didn't have to search in the east since he had come from there and so confined his attention to the north, west and south. Still nothing showed up on the horizon. It was late in the afternoon when Buck saw the fins of several sharks. They were off to starboard and paid no attention to the movement of the rafts. He was thankful for that.

The third day ended as it had begun with absolutely no change. The only difference was that the sky to the east and northeast was getting cloudy. He hoped that there wasn't a storm brewing as the rafts weren't any too stable with only one person in it. Another couple hundred pounds would make a difference in keeping the rafts more stable. He didn't have several hundred pounds, however. He could let some water into each raft if he had to weigh them down a bit. He would consider that option. The sunset was not as spectacular as the last two nights giving Buck the feeling that maybe change was on the way. He hoped it was the right kind of change.

Day four was cloudy and a few degrees cooler because the sun was partially covered. The sky to the west was clear but by the end of the day that might not be so. Also the wind had picked up and was blowing again from the northeast. Searching the sky was now part of the routine, followed by exercises, something to eat and more searching. The rafts moved west and Buck tried to steer them toward the northwest. He felt that he was going in that direction although he was probably going two miles to the northwest for every one mile he moved to the west. The swells of the waves were perceptible and Buck climbed into the second raft to make sure everything was stowed away or tied down. He did the same thing in the bigger raft, although he didn't take down his homemade sail.

It was just after three by his watch that Buck noticed something on the horizon. But with the seas so choppy and the swells becoming more ominous he found it difficult to stand up in the raft to get a better view. Nevertheless, he did and was able to see, for just a few seconds, a line of trees on the horizon. The direction was a bit north of northwest and Buck was concerned that maybe he might be blown past the island. He took down the sail, put on his life jacket and used the paddle to move in the direction he wished to go. He had to cut across the waves and the wind was hitting him on his right arm. At the top of a swell he could see the island but often for only a second. He put his heart into paddling and wondered if he would make the island before nightfall or would the storm blow him past the island.

After an hour of paddling, his arms were tired as was his back. He waited for a lull in the wind and on the crest of a wave he stood up and saw the island much more clearly. It wasn't all that big but it was only a mile or so away. He was heartened and thrilled that he might be able to get off the ocean before the storm and have solid earth beneath his feet. He renewed his efforts and soon could see the island with every stroke of the paddle. He could also see that waves were crashing over coral in several spots and that could create a problem at best for his raft or disaster at worse. He was heading toward the southeast section of the island and could see that the waves were relatively calm on the western side of the island. He paddled so that he would miss the coral on the south and southeast and stayed clear of the island until he was in the lea on the west. He saw coral there but it was several feet below the surface even when the rafts were at their lowest. As Buck moved closer to the island the wind lost its force and he was able to make good headway. He didn't take his eyes off the water for

47

a moment, fearing that the rafts could be chewed up on the coral if he let down his guard.

About ten feet from shore Buck stepped into the water up to his waist. Feeling solid earth felt great. He quickly got the rafts up to the beach and moved them up on the sand away from the surf. He had no idea where he was, or where it would be wise to set up camp. Then he chuckled to himself that he had a wonderful problem that he knew he could handle. He took a ten minute tour of the immediate area and figured that where he was would be as good a place as any. He pulled the rafts up to the tree line and started to set up a camp using the rafts as a tent.

Chapter 12

Sunday, November 22nd began with a beautiful sunrise which Buck couldn't see because he was on the western side of the island. For him the day dawned warm and beautiful. It had rained during the night and he was annoyed with himself that he didn't think to catch some rain water. That would have been smart and he wouldn't forget next time.

First on the agenda was a trip around the island. He got the binoculars and after popping a ration bar in his mouth and taking one of the canteens of water with him he set out toward the south and the area he tried to avoid the day before. He knew the island was not very large but as he started to walk he became convinced that it was even smaller than he first supposed. At the southern tip he noticed the coral and was glad he avoided landing there. He spotted coral reefs on the entire eastern side of the island. As he looked inland he knew he was on a volcanic island. The rock was extremely porous, almost like sandstone, the beaches were beautiful, yellow and like a picture postcard. There were coconut trees on all sides of the island, probably because the winds blew from one direction in the winter and another direction in the summer. He picked up a coconut and decided that he would have one for his second breakfast.

It took about an hour to leisurely walk the perimeter of the entire island. The center of the island wasn't very high, but would give a better view of the ocean He wanted to know if any other island existed within sight. But that would have to be left for another day. Buck used the awl on his knife to cut a hole in the coconut and another hole to allow the milk inside to drain into his mouth. It tasted so good. He then used another coconut to break the first and ate some of the meat inside. It was nice to have a change in diet even though no one would or could live on coconuts.

Buck used the smaller raft as his home and the larger raft as the roof. He figured that if it rained again he would use the larger raft to collect the rainwater and he would crawl under the other raft to keep from getting wet. He also began to think about catching fish. There was a fishing kit in one of the compartments of the raft and he set it up to catch some fish. He had no bait so he looked around to see what he could use. He remembered that he saw a dead fish washed up on the beach not too far away and decided to use that fish for bait. Before the afternoon was over he caught a white fish. He built a fire using one of the matches in the survival kit and put some rocks around the fire to confine it and keep the fire warm. Since he had no way to cook the fish he wrapped it in palm tree leaves, buried it with sand and moved the coals over the sand. He then moved his rocks. For supper he had a nice home cooked meal. He noticed that one side of the fish was cooked well and the other side needed to be cooked a bit more. Next time he would remedy that. This particular fish was also very boney. If fish was going to be a good portion of his diet, he would have to choose a tastier fish and cook it better.

The rest of the day was spent setting up and locating everything that was in both rafts. He opened up every compartment and pocket and emptied everything into the big raft. Then he decided where he wanted them to be and made a special effort to remember where they were. The flares and mirror always needed to be handy. As the sun set on this Sunday, he gave thanks for how lucky he was.

The next day was also a day of exploration. On the trip around the island there was a small inlet near the northern tip. Buck decided to go to the inlet for the purpose of fishing. On his way toward that spot he found a nice long straight stick that he sharpened with his knife. He was hoping that it would be easier to spear a fish. He saw several in the inlet and Buck wanted to improve his ability. It wasn't as easy as he thought it would be. The fish weren't where they appeared to the human eye. Buck had to study how his spear bent when it was in water. He figured out where he would have to aim if he had any reasonable chance to spear the fish. Finally he had success and lunch was secured.

In the afternoon, after a siesta, Buck put on his boots and climbed the hill that was the center of the island. Trees covered the hill but here and there he would have an unobstructed view of the ocean. Then he found a tree that was fairly easy to climb and he did so. He used the binoculars but the atmosphere was more humid than on most days and so the viewing distance was shortened. The tree allowed for a good view of most of the horizon. He thought that if he did this right after a rain he probably could get his best view of the distant horizon. It appeared now that the horizon was fuzzy and not as sharp as it was the day before. He was confident that he would get another chance.

Coming down the hill he saw a branch that would make a good spear. The end of the branch forked into three prongs, making it a much more effective fishing spear. Buck cut the branch and was anxious to sharpen it and test it out.

On the way back to the rafts he wondered if he should keep track of the days. He remembered that they left the base on the 17th and were shot down on the 18th of November, a Wednesday. He started to figure the days and he began to realize that if he didn't keep track soon he would be hopelessly lost as to the day of the week and the day of the month. Was that important? No. Except that he wanted to know. He wanted to know when it was Sunday so he could figure out what everyone was doing back home. He decided to determine what day it was and to make a calendar. He first figured the days since the plane got shot down by making marks in the sand. He went over the days several times and was certain that he didn't miss a day. Then he got one of the paddles. He could make many marks on one paddle and if he made them small enough a paddle could easily account for a year, maybe more. So with a pen he wrote the letters SMTWTFS across the top to represent the days of the week. He put an 18 under the W. He made a mark for each day and only wrote the numbers for the first S representing Sunday. Pleased with the format he used the knife to carve his marks into the paddle.

He tried out his new spear and was successful on the first try. He also liked the second fish much better than the first since he was able to cook it better. It also had fewer bones and sweeter meat. He now kept a fire going all day even if it was only coals. It made it much easier to start in the evening. With so much to do and so many decisions that needed to be made, Buck's mind was kept busy and his third day on the island came to a quiet close. As the sun was setting he made his mark on the paddle. It was November 24th.

The next morning he decided to try his skill again at spearing fish. Armed with his new weapon he walked to the inlet and spotted three fish in the cove. He saw a fish like the one he ate the day before and decided that he would get that one. This time it was a lot easier with the three pronged tool. He waited for the fish to come toward him and he knew just where to aim. He got that fish also on the first try.

He was so intense on learning this new skill that he didn't hear the motor. When he did, he saw a small boat coming from the north toward him. His first instinct was to get the mirror from his shirt pocket and signal. Then he realized he was in shadow and the boat might be a Japanese patrol boat. He got out of the water and squatted behind a fern. He was confident that he wasn't spotted. As the boat turned to avoid the coral and went toward the eastern side of the island, the flag of the rising sun was clearly visible. Two soldiers were using binoculars to search the island.

All of a sudden it hit Buck that the fire probably would be smoking and the rafts were clearly visible on the sand. He waited for the patrol boat to round the point and get out of sight. He then used the water in the inlet as his path to the ocean and ran as fast as he could along the western shoreline. He stayed as close to the water as possible so as not to leave footprints. Arriving at the campsite in a few minutes he quickly covered the fire with sand using the paddle as a shovel. Then he pulled the rafts back up into the bushes. This side of the island was still in shadow allowing the black rafts to blend in with the background. He looked critically at the campsite and except for his recent footsteps everything looked natural. He got a branch and smoothed out the sand from the shoreline to the bushes and retreated into a stand of mangrove trees and dark tropical bushes.

The patrol boat arrived in about five minutes. Buck had his binoculars and watched the two soldiers on the boat. They acted as if the island held no attraction for anybody and were careless in their inspection. They gave the campsite only perfunctory observation and moved on. Buck realized that his heart was beating very loud. Once the patrol boat passed he started to relax. He watched the boat pick up speed and head north. He was certain that they would report to their superiors that the little island was uninhabited.

Buck realized that he just had a close call. What if the Japanese saw footsteps on the beach or saw the fire? He knew he would be dead by now or running for his life. What if they went around the western side of the island instead of the eastern? They wouldn't miss the fire and life rafts that were sitting on the beach. He didn't want to think of what would have happened. What would he need to do now to make sure that he wasn't found by the Japanese? He could not leave all his stuff out in the open if he was to survive. He would have to find a more unobtrusive place where he could move his equipment. Since he left the spear in the fish in the small cove he decided to walk back to the north end of the island and retrieve the fish and the weapon. He might walk the island to find a more suitable place to reside.

Having found the fish where he left it, he wrapped it in some palm tree leaves and continued his walk toward the eastern end of the island. There the wind was stronger and the early morning sun touched the island there first. The coral was closer to the surface on that side and in November, the waves were bigger. He continued walking and near the northwestern portion of the island decided to look at that area more closely. He only went past the mangroves from the beach and wondered what was behind the grove.

After lunch Buck explored the section of mangroves. Now when he walked the beach he walked where the waves would wash away his footsteps and entered the beach where the water came right up to the vegetation, allowing him to step right into the water. He hadn't worn his boots since he took them off in the raft immediately after the plane was destroyed. He didn't need them now but knew that there would be an occasion when he would need them.

The mangrove stand was fairly extensive and not easy to pass through. It came right to the waters edge and he would have to time the waves correctly to cross in front of them without getting his feet wet. Behind the grove was a thicket of berries that Buck didn't realize were there. He found that they were edible. Then behind the berries was a rocky hill that was very heavily wooded. The trees were still relatively small and bushes and tropical ferns covered the ground. Anyone passing by would definitely choose the beach passage rather than trying to scramble over the rocky hill and crawl through the low plants and berry bushes. This might be a good place to hide the equipment and set up a camp, he thought. So far this was the best location.

That afternoon he decided that he would make the move to the northwest part of the island. He began by moving the two rafts to the water and then packing everything in the small one. He cleaned up behind himself, taking extra care to make it look like no one was ever there. Last of all he used a branch to erase his footprints. He then paddled to the mangrove stand and reversed the process. He carried the equipment first, then the larger raft and found a sheltered place among the smaller plants and bushes on the ground. It was on a slightly raised piece of ground and he could see a fairly large portion of the ocean, albeit between the mangrove trees. He knew that he could see out much better than anyone could see in. Transferring the equipment he came upon the flares and the flare gun and decided that it might be best to carry the gun with him along with the mirror should he see or hear an American plane. Buck noticed that it was clouding up and might bring a change in the weather so he decided to get his camp ready and to move the smaller raft to where it would gather some rain should there be a storm. He made a fire and cooked the fish just over the heat, using a green branch of a nearby bush. It worked just fine and the fish was cooked to perfection.

It wasn't until the middle of the night that the rains came. It rained hard for several hours and then it tapered off until the morning dawned clear and clean. The rain clouds could be seen disappearing to the southwest and the day was sparkling. Buck first filled the water canteens that he had already emptied. He made a mark on these so he would remember to filter the water when he got the chance. He knew it would be easy to run the water through sand to eliminate any foreign particles.

For now, he had something else on his mind. Buck figured he would get his best view from the top of the island and so grabbed his binoculars, put on his boots and took a trip to the top. He climbed the tree which he previously climbed and starting at the south he scanned the horizon. When he got to the north he stopped. Were his eyes playing tricks on him? No, there was something there. He braced himself and refocused the lenses again and was rewarded with the faintest line of trees. He could only guess that if he were on the beach he might not be able to see the trees. He guessed that it might be twenty or so miles to that island, just over the horizon. He made a note of the fact that the island was just a bit west of north.

Several concerns entered his head. Maybe that was where the patrol boat was stationed. Would he be walking right into the enemy camp? Could he paddle that far in a day? What if the island was no bigger than the one he was on? The more he thought about it the more determined he became that he would find the answer to all these questions. And he would do it today.

As he came down the hill toward the beach on the north, he couldn't see the new island. The island couldn't be seen from sea level. He checked the sea and the wind and found both to be peaceful. Buck was excited and was willing to take a chance with finding a larger island. Where he was he could find fish to eat, maybe a few berries and coconuts but the pickings were slim. Most any other island would be bigger and would have more food. He could hardly contain his excitement. He loaded the rafts and was on the water within a half hour, leaving nothing behind, not even his footprints.

Chapter 13

The day was long and Buck got tired from paddling. He didn't use the sail as the wind was very light. It wasn't until noon that he saw the first hint of trees on the horizon. He was excited but his excitement almost turned to exhaustion in his effort to get to the island. By three in the afternoon he still was seeing more trees and could not yet see the beach. The island was larger than he had expected. By five he saw the beach and realized that he still had several hours of paddling if he was to sleep on solid ground by the evening. By seven he was nearing the island and darkness was not too far away. He spotted the coral reefs and hoped that he would have enough light to reach the beach before he couldn't see these obstacles.

He avoided where the waves were breaking and found a spot where the water was moving faster but where the coral seemed to be deep. He was correct and was able to get into a quiet area on the southwest side of the island. He looked for a spot where the vegetation came to the water and landed there, lifting the rafts onto the grass and avoided leaving footsteps. A small clearing with grass on the ground was a good place to set up camp. He drank some water and ate one of the K-rations and needed no encouragement to fall asleep.

It was in the morning when he realized that he forgot to mark the paddle. As he did so he realized that the day he arrived on this island was the fourth Thursday in November, Thanksgiving Day. It was still Thanksgiving Day at home and so Buck blessed himself and formally thanked God for the blessings bestowed upon him.

Buck was not sure whether he would make his permanent home on this island. He didn't know if it was inhabited by the Japanese and if it was he would not want to stay there. He knew that he could always go back to his former island, although he didn't relish that thought. He put on his boots, his dark shirt and some mud on his face. He again felt like a soldier ready to meet the enemy. For now his mission was to avoid the enemy and explore the interior of the island. His immediate thought was that there didn't seem to be any trails nor any sign of human habitation.

The land began to rise as he moved inland and his walking became labored. Soon the hill turned into a mountain and much of the ascent was done by climbing. Buck was pleased that he had boots. The rock and hard terrain meant that he left no footprints and for that he was grateful. He reached the summit about lunchtime and ate one of his rations while sitting on a rock admiring the view. It was truly spectacular. He said a silent prayer that the island would not be inhabited. After drinking some water he aimed for the north side of the island. He found some trails caused by the natural formation of the rock. They were like shelves with trees and bushes growing where they were able to get a hold. Where possible he walked on these rocky paths but when he couldn't he was very careful not to leave a trail or snap a branch or break off a leaf. He knew that his boots would leave a mark unlike any boot the enemy might be wearing and if they were on the island he didn't want them to know that they had company.

He was surprised to find that the mountain had some caves. Several were small indentations that would allow a person to keep out of the weather. But there were a few that would allow a family to have shelter. He investigated several and saw no sign that anyone had ever visited them. He thought that it would be nice if he could find one to shelter himself. Well, maybe not up so high.

The day was pleasant enough and Buck enjoyed his hike. He especially enjoyed the sound of one bird which seemed to follow him. Yet he never got a good look at it. Several times he saw the bird fly off but couldn't see more than a silhouette. It had such an unusual and clear song that Buck hoped he would get to know this bird.

Coming down from the mountain took more care than one would expect. Disturbed rocks could give a visitor away just as fast as a broken limb on a tree. Then, too, there might be an enemy patrol or a camp just around the next rock. Having the high ground gave Buck some comfort since he knew that he would probably see them before they saw him and should he have to run he would be running straight or down and they would have to climb up. All of this ran through his head as he came down from the summit.

The terrain was not what he expected. One fairly high hill or mountain dominated the center of the island. As he was coming down he noticed that in front of him was a valley and a smaller hill that ran along the coast line from northwest to southeast. He stopped and listened for any sign of humans and then proceeded to climb down the hill.

Urinating is something you do and hardly give it a thought. However, this visit to the trees would not be forgotten. Buck decided to find a secluded spot, mainly out of habit. He was on a ledge that was beginning to narrow. He was peeing on a bush and his eye level reached another ledge with trees and bushes on it. As he stood there staring straight ahead he saw an opening in the rock. It looked large enough for a man to fit into but he had no idea how big it might be. When he was finished he climbed up to the ledge above him and pushing aside the bush was able to kneel in front of the opening. It looked large enough to hold a man and was certainly not easily accessible. Next time he would bring a flashlight and something to dig with to see if this could be a suitable place to hide. He looked around and saw a tree that dominated all the others. The tree would be his marker. It was north of the cave by about fifty feet. If he could find the tree he would be able to find the cave.

He continued his descent and was soon in the valley. He headed east between the other hill and came upon a lagoon. It was very quiet and hidden from the ocean for the most part. A critical eye from nearby could see that behind that little spit of rocky land was a small body of water that faced the morning sun. This might be a nice place to take up residence. Buck continued walking to the beach and found a spot where three rocks would allow him to reach the water without making prints. He took off his boots and negotiated the rocks to safely reach the water. He walked barefooted along the beach weaving through the last gasp of the breaking waves. He walked south toward where he had hidden the rafts. He made a note of the time and after an hour of walking he reached his destination. This island was considerably larger than the one he left. What was more important, as far as he could tell, it was uninhabited.

The next day Buck continued his exploration by walking along the western shore of the island. He took with him his knife, binoculars, some water and food and carried his boots around his neck. He experienced no surprises and after an hour was on the northernmost tip of the island. He climbed on a rock and searched the horizon for any other island in the area. From that vantage point none were seen. He then cut inland around the smaller of the two mountains and put on his boots. They would be needed to get to the cave he wanted to explore. In a very inaccessible part of the island which he believed would receive no visitors because of the dense vegetation, he cut a long stick that had four prongs at the tip. He wanted it for spearing and for probing his cave. He also wanted to take it from someplace where it would not be missed and no one could see that a branch was cut. This was certainly the spot.

He had a little difficulty locating the big tree because the valley was fairly covered with smaller trees. Finally in a bit of a clearing the tree was located and the climb made to the ledge where the cave was situated. On his hands and knees he used the flashlight to look inside. It went straight in, the full length of a man, then turned to the right. Buck got down on his elbows and crawled inside, keeping the flashlight ahead of him and his knife open in his right hand.

When he was fully inside, the flashlight illuminated a fairly large cave. It was approximately ten feet deep and eight feet wide. It was high enough to sit up in but not high enough to stand up straight. The floor was all sand and when Buck put his knife to the wall he found it was possible to get the wall to crumble fairly easily. Looking carefully at his find he determined that this would be the ideal place to store the rafts and all his other stuff. If anyone came it could be used as a great hiding place. Maybe he could dig out the floor a bit and widen the entrance. If he made the entrance wider, possibly a rock could be rolled over the entrance to make it all the harder to find.

Buck's mind was working overtime as he thought about all the possibilities. His concerns were to find food and water and these fairly soon. Maybe he could leave his stuff in this cave and sleep there at night and spend his days down by the lagoon. While he had plenty of matches now, if he used one a day, they would disappear fast and he didn't want to be without fire. He could capture water in one of the rafts and then filter it. There was bamboo on the island and the hollow tube could be filled with stones and sand and would filter his water nicely. As he sat in the darkness with light coming only from the entrance he decided that this cave would be a safe place for him and would shelter him and keep him unseen. He also decided that finding water and food would be the first two priorities, since shelter was solved. Tomorrow he would move the rafts to as close to the cave as he could get. There would need to be four or five trips up the mountain to make the move complete.

The trip back to the rafts was about an hour but there was no rushing. There was so much to think about and so many precautions to take. His thoughts were mainly of survival. The smaller island was probably safer but had little by way of food and water. Yet he knew he could survive there. The larger island was much more diversified and more likely to have water if it could be found. There would be more edible plants, the fish were plentiful and berries would almost certainly be in abundance. The downside was that this island might come into play in the war and possibly could be occupied by the Japanese at some stage. He reasoned that they had already checked out the island since he had seen their boat come from and go to the north when he was on the smaller island. In all probability it held no strategic value for them. He concluded that this is where he should be and where he would stay. With that thought he arrived back at the rafts.

As he was marking the paddle he noticed that another week had passed and that tomorrow was Sunday. It was a habit and obligation to go to Mass at St. Aidan's Catholic Church every Sunday when he was home and he now found that not being able to go with his family to worship was a ritual that he missed. He told himself that he would try to find some way to mark each Sunday, even if with only a prayer.

Chapter 14

Sunday dawned bright on the eastern side of the mountain and remained a bit cool on the western side. Buck searched the horizon and found no other islands within view. He easily found a coconut for breakfast. He was becoming aware that his supply of rations was dwindling and he would have to find some food to eat if he was to survive. He first kept his promise to thank God for all his blessings and he got down on his knees and said aloud that he was grateful for the protection he received. He asked God to protect his family and wondered if they were notified that his plane was lost. He prayed that they would survive this ordeal as he knew that he was loved by each of them and by Alice. He didn't know how long he prayed but it was probably ten or fifteen minutes and he was glad that he thanked God for taking care of him.

He moved the rafts from their hiding place and loaded them with all the equipment. Then he paddled the bigger raft with the smaller one trailing along behind. He found a spot that he thought was closest to the cave and took a load of stuff up the hill. Using the big tree as a marker was very helpful and he found the cave with no difficulty. Each trip he made using a different path, both to keep from leaving a trail and to explore the trees and plants. He discovered a tree with green fruit on it the size of melons and several of the fruit were lying on the ground. When he picked up the fruit it was sticky. He brought the melon like fruit back to the rafts and cut a piece. It wasn't all that bad, a bit fibrous but edible. He ate just a little in case it would make him sick. Then he took another load of his equipment up to the cave.

When it was time to move the rafts he realized that they were too big and heavy and clumsy to move through the brush. They would need to be deflated. He started with the larger one first and was surprised how much smaller it looked when all the air was out of it and all the emergency supplies out of the compartments and pockets. He folded it up but still found it to be quite heavy but not as bulky or cumbersome as he anticipated. As he climbed the hill his legs protested several times and he was forced to give them a rest. He realized that there were a few muscles that hadn't been used recently. When he arrived at the entrance to the cave he had to move the bushes aside to get the raft inside. The bushes snapped back to their original position quite well. He found that he could enter without disturbing the bushes if he bent his body a certain way. He also considered looking for a rock or several that he could put over the entrance after he was inside in case he needed to be completely hidden. For now he had another raft to get.

The rest of that Sunday was spent getting the last of his supplies to the cave. He used the hand pump that came with the raft to blow up the big raft so he would have a bed. Then he used the little raft to keep all the items he would need. He found a place to keep his flashlight handy, although he was reluctant to use the batteries, knowing that he only had six more after these were dead. His eyes adjusted to the light and with the afternoon sun shining through the small opening he seemed to have plenty of light. Putting the mirror in the sand to reflect sunlight into the cave also helped and he used several of the metal canteens to reflect some of the sun. At least in the afternoon he would be able to see.

Just before sundown he made one last trip to the water to make sure everything looked untouched. He did see a boot print in the sand that he had overlooked and was able to erase it with a piece of driftwood. On his way back up the hill he went by way of the fruit he found earlier and carefully brought several to the cave. Maybe these would help keep him alive.

The cave was comfortable but a bit cooler than the outdoor temperature and he was thankful for his flight jacket. He marked the paddle as was now his routine. For the first time in quite a while he was feeling safe and secure and filled with that knowledge he fell asleep quickly, covered with the flight jacket.

Buck was refreshed from his sleep and decided to walk up to the summit of the hill. He hadn't been there since he first explored the island. The view was magnificent and Buck found several other caves as he walked around. Most were good places to use to keep from getting wet but none were deep and hidden like the one he found. Still he wanted to know the island as well as possible in case he needed to hide. It became his conviction that he would never find another cave like the one he presently occupied.

The southern part of the island was very heavily covered with vegetation. It appeared more tropical and had a great variety of plants and bushes and all sorts of ferns. He even found some berries, although not all were ripe. He could hear and see birds flying but he had not come across an animal. He was especially attentive for snakes and wore his boots whenever he wasn't on the beach. When he saw a banana tree he was thrilled. They were smaller than the ones he sold in the grocery store and fairly green. He saw one bunch that looked like it was turning yellow and carefully cut it so the slice could not be seen. He thought to himself that he was being paranoid but better safe than sorry. While the island was much bigger than the first island, if the Japanese thought even one American soldier was on the island, they would search it foot by foot until he was found. He was making no mistake about that and taking no chances about leaving a trail.

As Buck was traveling on one of the ledges on the western side of the hill he noticed a clump of ferns. Ferns usually grew lower on the hill and he wondered what attracted them to this particular spot. As he knelt on the ground to examine the ferns his knee experienced a wet spot. Where would water come from? Behind the ferns he was able to see the wall of stone and spotted the wet spot. A few jabs with his knife and the removal of several wedges of rock provided him a tiny stream of water. Buck looked around and found a piece of bamboo and was easily able to sharpen it and make a trough to direct the water. He knew that he had found his spring. He filled up his canteen and inserted several of the wedges back into the hole, slowing the flow to a trickle. He would save the bamboo to fill up several other canteens. A brief memory of finding water from a spring when he was a scout quickly crossed his mind. He remembered watching as his Scoutmaster, Lou Sterling, opened a hole in the rock and produced water. It amazed him then and would save his life now.

Buck returned with his bananas and gathered the canteens that needed refilling. He tried a different route to the spring and almost got lost. He did, however, find a slab of stone that was round on one side and triangular on the other. He left what he was doing and decided to move the stone first. It was quite heavy and created a real strain on his legs bringing it back to the cave. It could be rolled into place and the triangular side would cover most of the entrance. He tried it several times and it was all that one could expect. It rolled easily and nicely disguised the opening. This would be the entrance stone that would make his cave much more secure and harder to locate.

He returned to the spring and filled the canteens. Back at the cave Buck crawled inside to see if he could operate the stone after he entered. He finally learned how to do it so that his hands weren't squeezed between the opening and the rock. He used the mirror to see how it looked outside and thought that maybe a bit more sand would make it look better. Once outside he put a small pile of sand off to the side but reachable with a stick. It was fairly easy to cover up the base of the rock and make it look very natural. He was most pleased with his day's work.

Buck hiked to the summit to watch the sun go down. The western sky had some stratus clouds and was pretty but the eastern sky was dark and threatening and the weather was moving from east to west. He figured that it would rain before the morning. That was fine with him as he would like to see the rain cover up any trail that he might have left. He was very careful but a rain would make everything look like new. A rain would provide insurance in case he left any tracks. Using his flashlight to avoid any missteps he returned to the cave. He decided that he would leave the rock in its open position and only close it if there was a need or if he felt threatened. He notched his paddle and made a note of the fact that in the morning it would be Tuesday, December 1, 1942.

Chapter 15

It rained during the night, a good hard rain. Because he was on the western side of the hill he didn't receive morning sun. He was awakened this day by voices. At first he thought he was dreaming but his heart jumped when he heard the voices of Japanese men. He moved to the entrance of the cave, rolled the rock over the entrance and used the stick to smooth the sand at the base of the rock. Nothing to do now but listen and wait.

The voices came and went. He heard no machine guns nor pistols but only the commands and communications of small patrols. At one time they were fairly close and Buck held his breath and said a silent prayer. Then the voices moved off. An hour didn't go by when voices could be heard again. Even a small island, such as this one, would take time to explore. The Japanese didn't realize it but they were trying to find a needle in a haystack. And they were not sure that the needle was even there. He prayed that they would not be successful.

The fruit found the day before was eaten. He felt confident that he could eat a larger portion since his stomach had no ill effects from the previous morsel. He found that it had a pleasant enough aroma and most of the fruit was sweet. Closer to the center it was tasteless and had a lot of fiber. But it was satisfying. He also nibbled on coconut and tried a banana. The banana was yellow but the fruit was not yet ripe so he pulled the skin around it and decided to wait a day or two. He had plenty of water and hoped the soldiers wouldn't be aware of the watering hole he found. With all the rain from the previous night he was quite certain they wouldn't notice just a little trickle of water coming from a rock.

The day passed slowly since he didn't feel safe to get out and about. Buck wanted to go outside and urinate but though it would be wiser to use a canteen in the cave. He could rinse it out later. Voices would occasionally filter through the trees and he began to consider that this exile might last for several days. For now all he could do was exercise, eat and sleep.

At dusk, Buck decided to venture outside. He quietly rolled the rock away from the entrance and eased himself out into the air, listening intently. Then he completed the motion and slowly stood. The sky was getting dark but he saw light from where he figured the lagoon would be located. He also heard the sound of a motor, probably a generator. There was electricity lighting up a string of lights. It looked like the Japanese would be here for awhile. No voices could be heard. It appeared that the search was called off for the night.

It was nice to stretch but for now it was too dangerous to venture far from his hideout. When he did finally go back in the cave he thought it would be best to move the rock back over the entrance and make his home as inconspicuous as possible. He made a J instead of his usual mark for the day, the J standing for Japanese. He also made several other markings on the paddle. X stood for the day he was shot down, L for landfall and B for big island. It wasn't much of a diary but it was meaningful to him.

Chapter 16

Alfred Schmerzle was standing in front of the A&P waiting to help a lady with her packages. Any lady, it didn't matter. He never asked for a tip but was always given something for carrying packages for the housewives and mothers who did the shopping. Alfred was deaf from birth but a pleasant, loving giant. The townspeople knew him and befriended him. It was the children who didn't understand his attempts at speech and were often frightened by him. Alfred was waiting patiently for his next request to help carry packages.

The black Ford was driving on Willis Avenue looking for Henry Street. They were almost through town and still hadn't found the street. They thought that maybe they passed it and just didn't see the sign. The two men in marine uniforms pulled over and called to Alfred.

"Hey fella, do you know where Henry Street is?"

Alfred answered as best he could but they didn't understand a word. So they kept repeating, "Henry Street, Henry Street."

Alfred had trouble speaking but he wasn't stupid. He walked over to the passenger side of the car and pointed to the nearest street. Then he held up three fingers and said as best he could, "One, two, three," as he pointed to the streets. The men in the car understood, thanked him and Alfred came to attention and saluted. He received a crisp salute from the marine in the passenger seat and a smile in return.

The Ford drove up Willis Avenue the three blocks to Henry Street, took a left and stopped at #23. It was four in the afternoon and both Martin and Lena were sitting in the kitchen. Mickey and Bobby were outside, probably up at the school playground. They heard the knock at the door and Martin, sensing Lena's fear, said that he would get it.

"Mr. and Mrs. Jones?"

"Yes, I'm Martin Jones." Lena had come into the living room. "This is my wife, Lena."

The two marines in dress blue uniforms stood relaxed but were still all business. No one had to tell Martin and Lena why they were there.

"We're here to inform you that your son's plane was shot down over the Pacific returning to base. Search planes were sent to the last known location with no results. We have no details but all men on board are presumed dead. The military have the men missing in action but that will soon be changed as there is little hope they will be found. I'm sorry."

The officer handed Martin an envelope with the official notification. Lena sat down.

"We want to express our deepest sympathy and that of the Marine Corps and the people of the United States. He could not have died for a more noble cause and we know that you are proud of him. A telephone number is included for you to call if you want us to help with any arrangements. There is a second number to answer any other question. You have our sincerest sympathy."

The two officers shook Martin's hand and nodded to Lena. Then they turned and walked out to the car to do the same thing again at another home on another day.

Neither said anything for a few moments. Then Lena said, "Martin, we've been officially notified that Buck's plane went down somewhere over the Pacific. That's all they know."

"They wouldn't have notified us if they weren't sure, Lena. We have to accept what is."

"What is, Martin, is that Buck is still alive. We can have a memorial service for him since there is no body or we can have a memorial Requiem Mass. I would rather the Mass. But between us, Martin, I know he is still alive and I will tell you, Bobby and Mickey that we should continue to pray for him just like we have been. If the marines want to say he's dead, that's their privilege. It just doesn't change what is."

"You seem very sure, Lena, and I so want to believe you. But I know that when the military say that he is dead they are ninety-nine percent sure. I'll go along with the Requiem Mass and we'll tell Bobby and Mickey that they told us he was dead but that we have some doubts. I'll tell them that we should all continue to pray for Buck as he may need our prayers more than ever. Can you accept that, Lena?"

"Yes, Martin, that would be OK. And I hope that I am right and that Buck returns home soon. For all of us."

When Bobby and Mickey came home from playing basketball on the playground they were told the news. All four held each other and said they were sorry and tears were flowing freely down Mickey's cheeks. Bobby was doing his best to keep his emotions under control.

Then Lena said, "I know what they told me and I accept God's will. I can't explain but I do believe that Buck is still alive and that one day you will see him again. I can't tell you how I know because I don't know myself. But in my prayers to God, he seems to be telling me that all will be right and that Buck will come home. I'll accept the fact that he is lost but I'll continue to pray for him."

"So will I, Mom," said Mickey. Bobby said that he would pray for him, too.

It wasn't missed on Martin that Lena said that Bobby and Mickey would see him again, not that they all would see him again. He wondered if Lena didn't have a direct line to heaven and knew something that no one else knew. She sure sounded like she did.

Chapter 17

Buck awoke the next morning on his own and not because of the sounds of Japanese soldiers. He cautiously opened the entrance and wormed his way partly outside. It was quiet. When he was completely outside and standing he could hear the generator and another motor. His curiosity was getting the best of him. He first wanted to make certain that they weren't still scouring the hills. He moved along the ledge above the cave because it went around the north side of the hill and looked out over the lagoon. He was relatively safe from anyone seeing him from above as the hill was fairly steep and no one would move that close to the edge where they could see him.

The ledge was also very thick with small trees and bushes and Buck determined that this spot would be a great lookout site. He found a rock where he could sit and have an unobstructed view of the lagoon. His first observation showed hundreds of soldiers standing around. Many of the tents were being taken down and it looked like they were preparing for departure. Soon a boat that reminded Buck of a landing craft arrived. It was then that he saw the bulldozer and he surmised that the landing craft was probably the boat that brought it ashore. He wondered why they would need a bulldozer. The craft was taking a good portion of the soldiers out to sea. Buck could see another larger boat waiting for them off shore even though the trees partially blocked the view. The same craft returned in a few minutes. The next large contingent got on board and left the island. It took two more trips to take the rest of the soldiers, their guns, tents and various other supplies out to the mother ship.

Buck was dying to see the entire operation but didn't think it was safe to leave his area. He concluded that the soldiers who left were on assignment to secure the island and now that they proclaimed the island secure it was time for them to leave. But why not everyone? And why was there a generator and some tents and now a bulldozer? As Buck thought about what was happening he came to the conclusion that they were going to build something. This little island was going to have some strategic value after all.

As Buck sat and watched the operation he saw a small group of five soldiers disappear toward the beach and the north end of the island. He surmised that they were a patrol and would walk the entire circumference of the island. Maybe he could get a view of them when they passed fairly close on the western side. He wanted to know their movements as that would help him to know when he could go to his spring for water or when he could get bananas or the fruit that he found. He also wanted to know what the Japanese were planning to do.

It also occurred to him that since there weren't too many people on the island now he could start identifying who did what. He would begin by identifying the leader of the patrol. He moved from his position overlooking the lagoon to a lower position. He had to walk a bit to find a view of the beach on the western side. He was just beginning to think that they weren't coming when he saw the five walking along the water's edge. From the fact that the man in the lead was wearing more insignia it could be assumed that he was the patrol leader. For now, until he learned otherwise, Buck decided that he would be the leader of what he would call alpha patrol. He returned to his nest overlooking the lagoon and tried to identify others. There was a tent and a wire was strung to it from the generator, suggesting that it had electricity. He saw another group of soldiers relaxing. Rifles were nearby, reminding him of alpha patrol. Maybe this could be beta patrol. They were in no rush and didn't seem to have anything to do. The bulldozer operator was starting to clear land in the valley between the two hills, working from the southeast toward the northwest. All the debris, roots and uprooted trees were being piled near the northwest corner of the island, next to the smaller hill.

There were a few tents in a brown green color back from the lagoon which were being set up for various functions. Boxes were outside and they were being opened and contents taken inside. Two men seemed to be assigned to each tent. One tent was probably being set up for radio operations and the second tent looked like some of the equipment was for first aid. Four men were setting up what seemed like a fairly large tent on a rise behind these tents. It too was a drab brown green but one had to admit that it blended right in with the color of the trees.

Buck watched until the group he designated alpha patrol, returned. He thought he would be able to recognize some of the men even if they were mixed with others. He saw a man come out of the tent and talk with the leader of the patrol and after a brief conversation he gathered his men and began his patrol of the perimeter. This leader was shorter and stockier and seemed to be a no nonsense kind of leader. He was getting ready to leave his perch when he saw a small craft come into view. It was not the same boat as before but was loaded with equipment and supplies and about ten more men. One of the pieces of equipment was a fork lift. He wondered what they would want with a fork lift. In a moment, after the fork lift was unloaded, it was used to unload the boxes and equipment on the craft. Buck admired their efficiency.

When Buck saw enough he looked at his watch and thought that if he hurried he could see beta patrol go past the spot on the western beach. He still wasn't in position when he saw them through the trees. They were moving at a slightly faster pace than the first patrol. Who would know when this information might be important.

Buck now felt relatively safe. He didn't think the patrols would be exploring the interior of the island but one could never tell when they might climb to the summit or one nature loving soldier would take a day hike to the interior. He couldn't kill a soldier without sealing his own fate. He knew that he would have to stay vigilant. Knowing how many people were working and what they were doing would give him some certainty as to his safety.

A visit to the spring to fill up canteens was a nice end to a productive day. The water reminded Buck that he hadn't had a bath for quite a while, that is since the day the PBY was shot down and he was in the ocean getting the rafts, and that could hardly be called a bath. There was soap in the survival kit and Buck thought that if he timed the patrol schedule correctly he might be able to take a bath right after one of the patrols was out of sight. Theoretically that would give him two hours and he estimated that he would only need five minutes. He knew it could be safely done. Maybe tomorrow would be a good day for these ablutions before too many more soldiers invaded the island. With all the people making tracks and damaging the foliage his trails wouldn't be noticed. Yet he knew he couldn't afford to be seen or even suspected of existing on the island. His mind worked to make sure that he planned properly and could safely take a bath in the ocean.

Chapter 18

It looked like a nice day for a swim. Buck decided to wash his underwear at the same time. He first had to see which patrol was up. From his perch overlooking the lagoon he saw the second patrol, the one designated as beta, getting ready to leave. Now where was alpha patrol? He didn't see any of them for a few moments. Beta patrol had already departed when he saw one of the men he recognized from alpha patrol coming from the large tent which he judged was the mess tent. Smoke was coming from one end so he was fairly certain of his assumption. Then he saw another soldier and knew that the second patrol was having a late breakfast.

He went back to the cave and gathered up the soap. How pleased he was to be able to bathe but knew that soap was going to be in short supply if he did this too often. Once wasn't too often. He watched from the opening overlooking the western beach and saw the short leader moving like he was in a rush. He watched everyone go past and made his way toward the beach. He looked for a spot where the water almost lapped the tree line. It took longer than he anticipated and he had to walk almost five minutes before he found a good spot to reach the water without leaving tracks.

Buck took off his boots and all his clothes. He took the mirror from his shirt pocket and left it on the grass. Then he put all his clothes in the surf to soak for a bit. He dove in and enjoyed his very brief swim in the winter water. The water was refreshing and it was nice to swim. He lathered up and dove in once more. He decided to wash his hair and this gave him a third chance to swim. He lathered his face, shaved by propping the mirror on a branch and rinsed off. While he had several weeks of growth on his face it wasn't too heavy as he was only eighteen and he didn't shave more than once a week.

He then washed his clothes and wrung them out as best he could. He made sure to clean up his footsteps on the beach and to leave the area undisturbed. With only his boots on he returned to the cave and hung his clothes over bushes and branches to dry. It was a nice feeling to be clean all over and he promised himself that he would bathe again soon.

Buck had a slight problem adjusting his watch to the time of day. The watch had to be wound each evening and several times he forgot to wind it and it stopped. He had to guess at the time. Then he realized that when the sun was directly overhead it was noon. He might be off a bit but probably not too much. By putting a stick in the ground he got a good idea of when the sun was overhead. About the only reason he needed a watch anyway was to time the patrols. It was a habit to look at one's watch and he felt lost without it.

After his clothes were dry he returned to his job of watching what was happening by the lagoon. He saw alpha patrol waiting their turn and drinking the Japanese version of coffee. Maybe it was coffee. It reminded Buck that he would like to start a fire and make a cup of coffee but he had no utensils. Nor would it be wise to build a fire.

The bulldozer operator was clearing a lot of land and a craft had landed more supplies and lumber on the bank of the lagoon. Buck also found a few new members of the work crew. Several of the men were waist deep in the water and it looked like they were getting ready to build a dock. In a half hour a small boat tied up to the bank and started driving the piles for the dock into the mud of the lagoon. The hammering went on all morning and was getting on Buck's nerves. He watched the patrol return and the other patrol set out. They always went counterclockwise and it always took two hours, give or take five minutes. It seemed fairly certain that this schedule could be relied on.

In the afternoon the bulldozer could be heard but not seen. It had to be on the south side of the lagoon. Buck left his spot and made his way over to the other side of the mountain, being careful to make sure no one or patrol was nearby or above him. He stealthily moved down the east side of the mountain until he could see the bulldozer. The operator was clearing a spot. He cleared a six foot wide path which then opened up to an area about fifty feet by one hundred feet. That area was now being leveled. While the operator was doing his work, a heavy set soldier was watching and occasionally giving directions. Buck had to move down the hill quite a bit to get a good view of the area but since it was very wooded and there were many bushes, he felt secure. It looked as if these were the only two workers in the area. Obviously they felt safe that they had the island to themselves as no weapons were visible. He wondered what was being planned for this site.

By mid afternoon the bulldozer was finished and returned to his other job of leveling the land between the mountains and piling up the debris down by the northern end. On the spot south of the lagoon a crew of six men came and installed a large tent on the leveled spot. The heavy man continued to order people around. By late afternoon the tent was installed and the heavy man looked pleased. His first piece of equipment to arrive by fork lift was a desk and chair which he had moved inside the tent to a shady spot. Buck had already sized him up as the quartermaster and a lazy one at that. This seemed to confirm it. Was the tent intended to store supplies? Maybe tomorrow he would find out for certain. The heavy man returned to the camp shortly after his desk arrived and seemed to be gone for the rest of the day. Buck gave him the name of Chuck for no reason other than he needed a name and Chuck seemed to fit. After returning to his cave he felt that everyday he was learning a little bit more but he still didn't know what the enemy was going to do with this island. He marked his paddle, as was now his habit, ate a banana, some coconut and a ration bar and felt free to drink plenty of water now that he had access to the spring.

The next three days were a carbon copy of the day before except for the fact that a small boat was often tied up at the dock and would make frequent trips to a freighter anchored off shore. The fork lift would then move the freight to the big tent south of the lagoon. Chuck would tell the operator of the fork lift where each box would go and would stand with his hands on his hips making sure it was placed where he wanted it to be. The sides of the tent were raised and tied up on the east and west side, allowing a breeze to flow through the tent. Buck's position was a bit too high but he could see most of the operation. When the operator left to pick up another load, Chuck used a crow bar to pry open the box and inspect the contents. Each day the tent got more crowded but the boxes were arranged in neat rows. Some were piled two or three boxes high and Chuck was checking off the boxes on his clipboard as they arrived. By the end of the third day the warehouse was filled and the freighter departed. Within hours another freighter arrived. The small boat remained.

While the warehouse was being filled, the bulldozer operator was continuing to level off the large field between the two hills. It was the size of a football field or larger, although it seemed longer than wide. Buck wondered what was going to be built on that field and what it would be used for. Maybe it would be a camp. All he could do was wait and see.

The small craft ferried cement bag like containers to the dock to be moved by the forklift. They were obviously heavy because the forklift struggled with the weight. These bags were moved along the edge of the field near the northern hill and dropped every few feet. Workers cut the bags and raked gravel in a straight line the entire length of the field from the dock to the debris piled up at the northwest end. The dozer would then drive over the roadway and make sure the path was level and firm. The forklift then laid out more bags of gravel at a ninety degree angle from the main path. The field was beginning to look like a giant comb. The new paths were wide enough for the fork lift but not the dozer. It was becoming obvious that they were planning to store something here and whatever it was needed a lot of space.

As the setting sun cast long shadows on the field, Buck knew that he would have to wait another day before the mystery was solved. He went back to his cave and realized that it was Sunday and he hadn't kept his promise to pray each Sunday. He prayed that he could somehow play a significant part in bringing the war to a swifter end. He told the Lord that he was getting tired of all the inactivity and that he was anxious to help. He didn't know it then but those prayers would soon be answered.

Chapter 19

Monday, December 7th was the first anniversary of the attack on Pearl Harbor and the day he found out that his island was being made into a refueling base for the Japanese Navy. It would probably be a major refueling base for submarines. Even before he got to his position on the ledge overlooking the lagoon he saw barrels already stored in the field on pallets at the northernmost path. These had to be oil drums. The fork lift was busy taking the pallets off the small craft and delivering it to the field. It was obvious that this was going to take a good portion of the next few days to fill up the field with barrels.

Before Buck left he noticed workers covering up the debris piled on the edge of the northernmost part of the field. They were spreading huge camouflage nets over it as if it were artillery. Some of the camouflage was laid out next to each row on the field. They were intended to cover the drums of oil and the gravel paths when each row was filled. He could only imagine that the island would look unoccupied from the air.

Buck wondered what was happening at the warehouse and so moved his position to the eastern side of the hill. Chuck was sitting at his desk and several soldiers were lined up in front of it. He was checking their supply list, writing information on it and then sending a soldier to pick up whatever was requisitioned. When they found all their supplies, they checked in with Chuck and he signed off on whatever they took with them. He then tore off his copy and put it under a rock so it wouldn't blow away.

Chuck was fairly busy until about ten o'clock when the procession dwindled to a trickle. From ten until eleven there were only two soldiers needing supplies. By noon, Chuck left for the mess tent. Buck wanted to go into the warehouse and see what was available. He knew he was getting low on meals and he wondered what else Chuck had that he might need. He felt that he would have to see how long Chuck took at lunch before he raided the warehouse. An hour later the quartermaster ambled back to his desk. After a few minutes he put his head down on his hands and fell asleep.

Lunch for Buck was an airman's lunch, a bar of rations and some water. He didn't see anyone come to the tent while he was there. At three he returned to his other position and observed the drums being stacked on the field. There were several aisles already filled up and covered with camouflage. They still had a long way to go. He could see no more advantage in observing so he went back to his spot to observe the quartermaster. He was most anxious to visit the warehouse and see what was available but knew that being caught or even seen could spell disaster. From what he could observe, Chuck hardly ever looked at the supplies but made each soldier find what was requisitioned and then Chuck would check to make certain that he got the correct supplies. The idea that he could visit the warehouse the next day was exhilarating. Buck could hardly wait.

The next morning with binoculars, water and some rations, Buck left the cave and observed the lagoon. He was surprised at how rapidly that operation was progressing. A dozen or so aisles were already covered and the field was filling up fast. The warehouse was busy at this early hour but by ten only one soldier could be seen. Chuck kept busy with paperwork when no one was there. He occasionally got up and walked around but never did anything strenuous. At about ten minutes to noon, he stretched and strolled to the mess tent. No one was in sight.

Buck moved along the tree line south until he could remain in the woods and come up on the back of the warehouse. He was in the open field only a few seconds and was sure he wasn't seen. He watched the camp for a few minutes to make sure his presence wasn't noticed. Then he quickly moved up and down the aisles seeing what was available, just like in a supermarket. There was everything here that a small town would need. His eyes saw so many things that he needed and wanted. First of all, food. He wasn't sure but he thought he found the G.I. equivalent of rations and took about twenty boxes of them. He saw soap and took two bars of that. He though he could use a blanket and did need something to carry everything in. He added the blanket. He found a box of matches and threw them in his homemade valise, as well as a few candles. Then he grabbed some more candles and thought it would be nice if he had sterno and could cook. He found some cooking supplies and took a pan and a pot and was pleased to see a small stove with containers that would provide heat. At least that is what he thought he was taking. His bag was getting heavy and knew that he was getting close to capacity. It was time to go. Along the way he spotted a bottle that looked like it might be juice so he added that to the blanket. He left the same way he came with the blanket over his shoulder, trying not to make noise. Once he started up the hill he knew he was home free. He also felt secure that he didn't take anything that would be missed and that he left no trail.

That was when he thought about his boots leaving an impression that was definitely not of Japanese markings. He couldn't go back and if he did just raking up his footsteps would be more noticeable than leaving the warehouse alone. He decided to bring everything back to the cave and then to observe Chuck's actions after lunch.

When Buck got back, Chuck had still not returned. When he finally did return he sat at his desk and took his afternoon nap. In the next hour one soldier came for some supplies but Chuck remained at his desk. Buck felt that everyone walking up and down the aisles in the morning would erase all trace of his boots. He would check that out the following morning. For now he felt lucky that his thievery was not discovered.

The field was about three quarters filled with oil drums. What could be done to blow up this supply depot once it was fully stocked? Buck was seeing a way he could contribute to the war effort and hurt the Japanese if he could destroy this base. Blowing up their depot would surely hurt them, but could it be done? If it could be done, could it be done without being killed in the process?

Buck sat on the ledge and began to ponder all the possibilities. He would have to get closer to the lagoon if he was to survey how the depot was situated. He wanted to observe if there were any trees or ground cover to allow him to move undetected to the oil drums. Then he would have to find a way to set fire to the drums. Once he got several burning he was certain that the heat would ignite all of them. He considered whether the wind could be a factor. He also wanted to know what it would take to get the oil to burn and would it be possible to light the fire and still get away. As he watched the barrels of oil steadily get stacked in the field, he realized how important this was to the Japanese war effort. He was convinced he found the reason he was spared in the loss of the PBY and its crew.

Back in the cave, Buck tried out his candle. He was thrilled with having some light once the sun had set. He decided to try out the juice that he got and had to use the corkscrew on his knife to open the bottle. It was then he found out that it was saki and not juice. While Buck didn't usually drink he considered making this an exception and so drank several ounces from the bottle. He put the cork on and decided that it could enhance his next meal. The cans he brought were sterno and he thought they would be good for heating water for coffee and tea and for cooking the fruit that he still couldn't identify. He also tried out one of the rations and while it wasn't to his taste, it was edible and filling and probably loaded with needed vitamins. He was thrilled with all his goodies and as he marked the paddle he noticed that it was December 8th. To him it was Christmas, regardless of the date. He covered himself with his new blanket and was soon asleep.

Chapter 20

Buck willed himself to wake up early and he woke before the sunrise. He considered it a luxury to have a hot cup of coffee with his rations. It was just getting light when he arrived at his spot overlooking the lagoon. Soldiers were awake and going into the mess tent. The camp was stirring but no work was as yet in progress. He made his way to his spot that overlooks the warehouse and was surprised to find Chuck already there, sitting at his desk and drinking something warm, as evidenced from the steam that was visible. Chuck evidently wanted to be at his position before the soldiers arrived. Maybe he was afraid that someone might steal from his supplies without his knowledge.

About fifteen minutes later the first soldier arrived and handed Chuck the requisition. He wrote something on it and the soldier retrieved the item or items. He showed his items to Chuck, was given the duplicate copy of the requisition and left the warehouse. Five minutes later the second soldier arrived, then the third and several more soldiers arrived minutes later. By now the inside of the warehouse would be covered with footprints, obliterating any that Buck made from his American boots. When he was satisfied that Chuck was unaware of his visit and that no one spotted the unusual markings of his boots, he left his hiding place and made his way toward the lagoon. The problem that he would have to solve was how he could steal again without leaving footprints.

He stayed behind the tree line as he moved toward the lagoon. Soldiers were moving toward the warehouse and others were moving back to the camp carrying their supplies. One soldier had a wheelbarrow filled with rakes and shovels. Where the trees were thin he had to move deeper into the woods. Eventually he neared the lagoon. From this view he could see all the tents and the small town that was carved out of the island. Until now all he saw was a small portion of it. There were no guards posted although it looked like alpha patrol was getting ready to make their trip around the island. He estimated that there were probably about fifty soldiers in all, perhaps a few more, still on the island.

From this view, with the camouflage covering almost all the oil drums, the camp looked benign. Buck took the long way around the camp making sure that he remained well hidden in the woods. He saw a path that went into the woods to a latrine. He made a note of its location. This was one spot he would want to avoid, especially in the morning. He climbed over a rise at the base of the hill and approached the field with the oil drums from the west. He was able to stay in the woods and get right next to the camouflage netting. Now he wished he had a container of some sort. He thought that if he could get a sample of the oil he could experiment with it to find out the best way to ignite it. He wanted to know if it was volatile and if so, how volatile? Would it explode when he lit it or could he make a fuse? How should he light it so he could get away? He needed a container in which to bring the oil home if he was going to answer these questions.

The path back to the cave from the end of the oil field was either steeply uphill or a more gradual but longer route. He choose the steeper route and it was exhausting. Once he reached the cave Buck drank from his canteen and emptied it. He then emptied the saki into his canteen, saving the cork and bottle. It was just too good and enjoyable to waste. He got out his knife and was relatively certain the awl on it would pierce the oil drums.

Satisfied that he was equipped to get a bottle full of oil, he felt it was time to get in a few provisions. He had enough water but could use several more pieces of the fruit that he found on the ground. And he knew a trip to the southern end of the island would take a good portion of the afternoon but he also wanted to stock up on some bananas. He planned to go down to the beach and would easily find a coconut. After his lunch he set out for the western side of the island. He tried to find the place where he took his bath so he could enter the water without leaving footprints. He hadn't timed the patrol so he didn't know if one had come by recently or was scheduled to come by. He would just have to chance it.

He found his spot and stepped into the water with his boots on. That was a mistake so he climbed out and took his boots off. He looked up and down the beach and saw a stand of coconuts toward the south and decided that he could get to them and was reasonably certain that he would find several coconuts. He entered the water, leaving his boots on the grass under a bush. He was about half way to the coconuts when he turned around and saw a patrol just rounding the northern bend. They were still a good distance away. He immediately fled into the bushes at the tree line, leaving a trail of footprints in the sand. A good wave wiped out the first three or four but there were still four left that were obvious. Quickly he looked for a long branch and found one that fitted the bill. He tried to cut through it but it wasn't as easy as he anticipated. Finally he had his branch, about seven feet long and was able to wipe out all but the farthest footprint. He stepped onto the beach and wiped out that last footstep, retreated to the grass and erased the other footsteps. He threw away the branch and looked at his job. It was not too good. If the patrol was observant they would see that the sand had recently been disturbed and was a different color. No footsteps were visible but the sand was disturbed. He could only pray that they weren't paying attention. He also could hear their voices and knew that he couldn't reach his boots. All he could do was retreat into the woods and hope that no one would notice.

As the patrol passed, Buck heard them talking and laughing. It was banter like you would hear from any soldier around the world, except the language was Japanese. They passed the boots without noticing them. As they passed Buck he recognized the leader from alpha patrol and held his breath that they weren't paying attention. One of the soldiers was telling a story or a joke and all seemed to be listening intently. They passed by the sand that was disturbed and their laughter could be heard after they were about twenty steps beyond. He let out a huge sigh of relief and offered up a short prayer for his good fortune. He then berated himself for being so careless.

After retrieving and putting on his boots, Buck got a coconut and made sure he covered his footprints. He took to higher ground and walked to where he remembered the bananas to be. He found the grove and was able to find a bunch that looked like it was ready to be harvested. He put the coconut inside his shirt, making him look like he was pregnant and carried the bananas in his arms. He was very pleased to be home without having been discovered and vowed that he would never be that careless again.

That evening at sunset he made his way to the northern end of the field. He watched and waited making sure that no one was in the area, that there were no guards posted and that he wouldn't be seen when he crawled toward the camouflage. When it was dark he made his way to the camouflage and quickly crawled under it. He was then able to crawl between two drums and eased himself in about three rows deep before the aisle became too small. He used his flashlight only when absolutely necessary. He put his knife with the awl blade exposed to the drum and gently tapped. It didn't sound too loud. He took off his shirt and used it to deaden the sound even more and this time he gave it a hard hit. It made a hole in the drum and oil began to leak out. He turned on the flashlight again and faced it toward the drum to see how best to get the oil into the bottle. Using his finger and holding the bottle with the other hand he managed to get the oil to trickle into the mouth of the bottle. He turned the flashlight off and was able to execute the maneuver by feel. He could sense the bottle getting heavier and when he thought it was about half full he turned on the light and cut a sliver of wood from the pallet to plug the hole. The oil stopped flowing. It didn't stop the flow completely but it would take a year for the oil to flow down to that level. Once the cork was in the bottle it was time to head home.

Buck stayed on his hands and knees until he got to the trees. He didn't want anyone spotting his footprints in the fresh dirt around the field. Then he used a piece of a branch to smooth over the prints he did leave. He made his way up the hill the long way since it was difficult to climb holding the bottle of oil in his slippery hands. Dropping it would mean he would have to make another trip to the oil drums. That he didn't want to do. The moon was in its first phase and provided some light but not too much. He was able to find his way back to the cave with little difficulty.

Buck couldn't wait to get started with his experiments. He first poured a small portion of the oil on a rock and tried to light it with a match. He was successful if he didn't put the flame right in the oil. He found after a few tries that the oil was not volatile but would burn well. He made a wick out of toilet paper, a roll of which he found in each raft. If he poured a few drops of oil on a square of toilet paper it would ignite easily and would flame up to ignite a larger pool of oil. This would be his wick for igniting the oil depot.

Buck then experimented with the candle. He found that the candle would burn without igniting the wick until the flame burned down to the wick. He was able to keep the moistened toilet paper where he wanted it to be by using some wax droppings to keep it in place. He would then experiment with how long the candle had to burn to give him a five minute head start before the depot would ignite. From start to finish it didn't take an hour to figure out the whole process and to be satisfied that his simple fuse would work each and every time. He also experimented with how much oil to put on the paper and found that a few drops would do the job well.

It was a good feeling to have a plan that looked like it couldn't help but succeed. Buck went over the plan many times and believed that there was little risk and a very high degree of probability that it would be successful. It was not in his nature to be smug but he felt that there was nothing that could stop him from blowing up the oil depot. What he didn't know was how the Japanese would react. Would they immediately suspect sabotage and search the island for the perpetrator? Maybe they would think it was an accident. Possibly someone would consider spontaneous combustion as a possibility. In any case, no one knew how the Japanese would react. At least the depot would be destroyed.

The more he thought about their reaction the more he thought that they would suspect that someone blew it up and would retaliate by searching the island inch by inch until he was found. That might be the price he would have to pay to hurt the enemy like he intended. The depot would be destroyed, however, and that would save many American lives. Whatever the cost it would have to be set on fire and destroyed.

Chapter 21

Chuck, whose real name was Takahashi Anzai, was told to expect an influx of troops and supplies. With the arrival of the 100 or so soldiers would come tents and equipment to sustain them. They were also bringing a supply of light artillery. Chuck was told that they would be setting up the tent camp south of his warehouse.

Chuck didn't like all the extra work that this would entail but he had more than enough room in his warehouse for all the new stuff. What he didn't like at all was that his quiet afternoons would be disturbed by the tents being located so close to his work. It meant that he might not be able to take his afternoon nap. He also found out that they were going to double the supply of oil on the island and submarines were being alerted to this new facility.

It seems to be a common trait of quartermasters that they want to know everything that is going on. The nature of their business requires them to talk with and interact with many people each day. They hear rumors and they ask questions and so often they are the best informed soldiers in the entire outfit. Most of this knowledge comes without effort. What Chuck found out was that they didn't want a large force on this small island. They needed a force to provide resistance should the Americans find out that this little island was a refueling stop for submarines. A small force could accidentally stumble on the island or in looking for a lost flyer, a plane could spot something out of place. That is why the oil drums were covered and from the air the island looked like it always did. Still some resistance might be needed should they come into contact with a small scouting party.

As Chuck looked at his warehouse he saw several rows of supplies that could be compacted and combined and he would have plenty of room for all the new stuff. If he needed to, he could combine plenty of other supplies to make room. He just had to reorganize it so that he knew where everything was and he didn't see that as a problem. If this quartermaster was anything, he was efficient. He would even admit to being lazy and a procrastinator, but never was he inefficient.

The only concern that Takahashi had was that the more military personnel on the island, the greater the chance that they would attract attention. He hoped that all the camouflage would keep the island looking untouched and that it would not be found by the Americans. He liked his life on this particular island and if one had to be in a war, a soldier could do worse.

Two soldiers came to his tent, one being an officer and Takahashi stood and saluted. He gave the officer and his assistant a tour of the facility and told him that he was generously supplied up until now. The officer assured him that nothing would be lacking with the arrival of the new troops. They toured the warehouse then left for the area south of the warehouse. That was the area set aside for tents. It looked to Chuck like the tents would be right at the tree line and not out in the open. When the tents were erected the next day that was where they were situated.

Chapter 22

The noise that greeted Buck the next day was confusing. Looking over the lagoon there was a lot of activity and many more soldiers than previously. There were two fork lifts and the bulldozer was no where to be seen. There were now two shallow craft ferrying materials from a destroyer in the harbor. A second boat, a freighter, was waiting its turn. Buck tried to count the new soldiers but because they kept moving, he couldn't get an accurate count. He would guess that there were about one hundred new soldiers. He also noticed some machine guns and small artillery being unloaded. One of the fork lifts was unloading sandbags which would probably be used to protect the machine guns.

He noticed that groups of soldiers were being moved to different parts of the island. A group of ten soldiers would board the craft with machine guns, sandbags and boxes of what appeared to be ammunition. They would probably be dropped off at strategic spots on the island. Buck was immediately apprehensive that his days of freely roaming the interior of the island were over and that any movement would have to be done with extreme care. With this many soldiers there were so many possibilities that a patrol would turn up where it was least expected. On his way back to the cave Buck heard voices above him. He saw some soldiers setting up a post on the top of the hill. He knew that this would restrict his free movement. It wouldn't stop it, but would definitely curtail some of his ability to wander freely. He also wondered if the machine gun nests would be manned at night.

As the day wore on he saw that a machine gun post was set up near where he took his only bath. It looked as if he could walk to his spring for some water but would have to be careful that those on the top of the hill were in their nest and not walking about. He had free access to his ledge overlooking the lagoon, providing he kept his head down so as not to be seen from above. In an afternoon trip to the ledge he saw that the fork lifts were adding new drums to the ones already there. They were piling them two high.

As he sat there watching both fork lifts carry the drums he counted twenty drums in each line. That made forty drums per path. And presently there were twenty paths. With the camouflage off the first path he could get an accurate count. He figured that there were eight hundred drums stockpiled already and if they doubled the number by stacking them two high his calculations reached sixteen hundred barrels of oil. That would supply more submarines than Buck cared to think about. By blowing up the depot, the Japanese would be deprived of a base for refueling their submarines. That would definitely put a dent in their plans, at least Buck hoped it would.

On the way back to the cave it became clear that it would be smart to let the Japanese unload all the oil that they were going to unload. It was just as easy to blow up sixteen hundred barrels of oil as to blow up one. The only difference would be in the explosion it would make. Sixteen hundred barrels of oil exploding and lighting up the sky might bring American planes and troops to the rescue. That was a prospect that enlightened Buck's spirits. So while it was difficult to be patient, waiting would increase the amount of oil that would be destroyed. So the plan to immediately blow up the depot was put on hold.

That evening Buck decided to make a very cautious trip to the oil depot to see if any patrols were guarding it and also to find out what the enemy was doing behind the hill. When it was dark and just before the moon was making an appearance, he went down the short way to the valley, armed with only his binoculars. He would move a short distance, stop, listen and look for anyone on patrol or guard duty. He was most afraid that he might accidentally come upon a soldier using the woods for a latrine. He was concerned that he might not see him behind a tree and could walk up to him without even noticing the soldier. And he was well aware that he wasn't armed and the soldier would be. He would just have to be cautious and take his time.

He moved from tree to tree along a good portion of the oil field and was convinced that they were looking out to sea, not inward. He worked his way over to the pile of debris at the end of the oil field and moved along that line in shadow toward the smaller hill. He got down low and very quietly made his way up the hill.

At the top of a rise he was able to see some light out in the water. Using the binoculars he saw a submarine. One of the craft that usually stayed tied to the pier in the lagoon was docked up to it. It was obvious that the sub was being refueled even though one could not see the entire operation. It was quiet, with just the barest amount of light and it wasn't but a few minutes before the craft was headed back to the lagoon and the sub was underway to deeper water.

It surprised him when he saw the light from a cigarette, about forty feet ahead of him. The soldier said something to his buddy and the two laughed. He was glad he wasn't any closer. He watched and with the light from the moon was able to make out the silhouette of a machine gun resting on sand bags. Camouflage netting was draped over some small trees, making the guns invisible from the air. The machine guns would, however, have a good view of the sea and could make it extremely difficult if a force tried to land on the northern beach. This was probably true of all the gun emplacements. After a good inspection of their nest, Buck made a most careful retreat. When he got to the debris he crawled to keep out of the moonlight. It surprised him how bright the moon had become in just an hour's time.

As he crawled and was almost to the end of the debris, he felt a sharp pain in his right quadriceps. It stopped him for a moment and it took tremendous restraint to keep from screaming. He was impaled on a broken off piece of timber from one of the trees piled up at the end of the field. He didn't want to use his flashlight and it was only with some difficulty and a lot of pain that he was able to extricate himself. The leg was bleeding badly and he knew that he would have to stop the flow if he was to make it back to his cave. He took off his belt and wrapped it twice around his thigh before buckling the belt. That stopped the bleeding, at least temporarily. Then he moved as best he could toward the cave.

He had to go the longer way home since it would take more strength than he had to climb the steeper path up the hill. It was bad enough walking up a fairly steep hill but at least he was able to do it. His mind told him that this was a very bad stroke of luck but wouldn't ruin his operation. All he needed now was to get some sleep and for his leg to heal.

Back in the cave he covered the entrance way with the rock and turned on the flashlight to see how bad his leg was. It had bled some and made a mess of his trousers. He was grateful for the bleeding and hoped that the flow of blood would clean the wound. It hurt to touch and he admitted to himself that the splinter of wood had pierced his leg deeply. He hoped that it wouldn't get infected. After washing it and covering it with a piece of gauze from the medical kit he decided that sleep was the best medicine. The leg throbbed and he wished that he had some saki to kill the pain. It wasn't until several hours later that he finally drifted off to sleep.

Chapter 23

When he awoke the next morning his leg was still throbbing, was swollen and extremely stiff. He had a leisurely breakfast especially enjoying the luxury of a cup of hot coffee. This was a day for him to recover and he had no intention of doing anything that would slow that process. He was convinced that now was the time to attack the depot before any more troops arrived or before they blocked his entry to the field by putting up a fence or moving some operation nearby. He also didn't want any more submarines using this facility. So he lolled around all day, sleeping when the spirit moved him and generally resting. By the evening he pronounced the leg no better. He was beginning to get worried. It would be wise to give it another day. With that thought in mind he changed the bandage and tried to get some sleep.

In the morning his leg felt hot to touch and there were red infection lines running down some of the blood vessels. All day he thought about his plight. He considered that this infection might kill him and that all the planning would be for nothing. If he waited several days he might not recover. If he went tonight he probably was still capable of moving that distance and could probably get back to the cave. He would definitely have to go the long way. He also decided that he needed a ten minute fuse. Five minutes would not be enough.

He rested as much as possible all day and didn't want to admit even to himself that he was getting worse. He knew that he needed medical attention and none was available. He gathered his candle, flashlight, knife, toilet paper and tried to sleep. His plan now was to wait until it was totally dark yet before the moon would make its appearance. On such a clear night the moon could ruin everything because it was becoming brighter each night. He needed to be back before the moon was up which he estimated would be after ten that night. He also needed to be back before the depot exploded or at least be very close to the cave.

Even though he was pumped with adrenaline he was sick enough that he was able to sleep. At dusk he sat outside the cave and said a prayer that all would go well. He watched a beautiful sunset and made a notch in his paddle. He put on a little soot from the edge of the sterno stove on his face and the back of his hands to make his skin less visible. Then he waited.

When it was totally dark he moved awkwardly down the hill. He went the longer way with all his senses on alert. Yet the sense that was serving him the most was that of pain. He was hurting and had to will each painful step. He recognized that he was dizzy and it took a real effort to keep his balance and not fall. When he reached the base of the hill he stopped to listen for any sound. The silence was total except for the generator. He moved forward.

As he came out of the tree line, not far from the field of barrels, he crawled, using his hands as feelers. It was dark when he reached the first row of barrels, not too far from the center of the field. He crawled under the camouflage and felt secure for the first time. If the camouflage could keep the enemy from seeing what was underneath it could keep them from seeing in as well.

He wedged his way in and found a large enough spot to begin the operation. He punched a hole with the awl tool on the knife in the bottom of the barrel and another in the top. The stream of oil was flooding the ground and starting to pool. The smell of oil was strong but he made the holes so that the oil would spurt out away from himself. He then put holes in a few more barrels, again facing them away from him. He lit a match and lit the candle. He put the toilet paper around the candle and used some of the wax to hold it in place like he practiced. He was quite certain that it would take ten minutes or so to reach the paper. He placed a few drops of oil on the paper. He knew not to put too much but just enough to start a nice fire and let the paper touch the oil that was pooling on the ground. A few drops of wax secured the candle to a wooden pallet. He gathered up his flashlight and knife, took one last look to make sure that he had done everything correctly, then stuck his head out from under the camouflage.

He knew he made some tracks coming in and would make some more going out. He used a small stick to cover up behind himself as he crawled to the tree line. It took longer than he thought but he wanted the ground to look normal. He was very weak and once he had to rest after having gone only twenty feet. He looked back at the field and because he knew where to look, saw the warm glow of the candle. That meant that time was ticking and he needed to get up the hill and to the safety of the cave. He pressed on. He kept waiting to see the sky light up but it remained dark. He was now half way up the hill, only a few minutes from safety and still no fire. He stopped for a moment and began to wonder if perhaps he didn't do it right. It was too late. If he made a mistake he would have to return another night. His strength was gone.

Within sight of the cave he saw the glow from the oil ignited on the ground. From a nice fire it quickly spread and became a roaring fire. Then the first barrel exploded, followed by the second, third and several more together. Buck stood at the entrance to the cave too shocked to move. He did it. He blew up the enemy's oil depot. The explosions continued and the entire sky was filled with light. Night became day and he was astonished at the explosions and the extent of the fire. He hoped the Americans would see the explosion and would come and investigate.

He squirmed his way inside and lit a candle. He replaced the rock carefully over the entrance. He then saw that his pants leg was dark with fresh blood and his leg was throbbing. He just wanted to put down his head and sleep even though he was exhilarated with the success of the evening. He determined that he would have to replace the bandage regardless of how tired he was. As he took off the old bandage the wound started bleeding again. He put on a new bandage and used his belt to keep direct pressure on the wound. He laid his head against the side of the cave and was asleep in a minute. The uncomfortable position woke him up shortly and he replaced the bandage again, putting some medicine on it. He ate a ration bar, drank some water, blew out the candle and laid down properly. Now he could take his well earned rest.

Chapter 24

Takahashi had just finished eating in the mess tent and was now playing cards with some of his buddies in that same tent. He had his back to the tent flap when someone said that it was glowing red outside. Then they heard the explosions and everyone left their cards to see what was causing such a commotion. As the explosions came closer to their tent and more barrels of oil lit up the sky the air raid alarm was sounded. Takahashi's first thought was that this had to be caused by an air raid. Yet he hadn't heard any aircraft.

Everyone had somewhere to go and things to do when the air raid siren was sounded. Soldiers, still putting on a shirt in some cases, were running to their stations. Takahashi hurried toward the warehouse. He met several soldiers along the way and asked what was happening. They said the words "air raid" and kept on running.

The barrels were now about fifty percent exploded and the tree line near the field was on fire. It was as bright as day. As the barrels on the northern end of the island exploded and got near the pile of debris, it too became engulfed. Soldiers were moving away from the field and the machine gun nests were being abandoned. No matter what their assignment it was impossible to compete with the heat from the conflagration. Some were heading toward the smaller hill and others toward the ocean itself. No one wanted to be near the inferno. The fire burned like no one had ever seen before nor could anyone know for certain what caused it. The consensus was that the Americans did it, probably with a lucky bomb.

The commanding officer left the mess tent and headed for the radio shack. He asked the operator to get him headquarters. He spoke quickly and urgently telling headquarters that the entire island was being consumed with the fire and that all the oil supplies would be destroyed shortly. He was told to get everyone ready to abandon the island by morning as that was how long it would take to get a ship to that location. It was assumed that the Americans would surely see the fire and would soon investigate. All they could do now was hope to escape. Feeling the heat from the fire on his face he hurried from the radio room.

The commanding officer used the loud speaker to tell everyone to abandon the island and to destroy any equipment or materials that could be used by the enemy. He sent the two craft to warn those who were on the southern end of the island and to bring them back with their equipment. One of the small boats went around the northern end and the other boat took the route to the south. Those on the top of the hill could see the fire and hear the explosions and took it upon themselves to abandon their post. They brought their machine gun and ammunition with them.

Takahashi arrived at the warehouse and looked at everything that was there. Most of the supplies were of little value to the enemy. The Americans would never wear Japanese uniforms and all the guns and ammunitions were kept in a tent on the other side of the lagoon. He was attempting to find items that needed to be destroyed but was having trouble doing so. He didn't mind giving out materials and supplies to those who needed them but he didn't want to just destroy all these items. He concluded that everything in the tent had no strategic value.

"Anzai, you are needed at the pier," shouted an officer. Takahashi was happy to give up the task of choosing what needed to be destroyed and what should remain. He left the tent immediately.

Chapter 25

Captain Paul Walker was on duty that evening on the Aircraft Carrier Hornet. He was handed a message telling him that a PBY located a big fire in the Caroline Islands. Coordinates were given and it was suggested that planes from the Hornet investigate. Walker made a few inquiries and was told that no allied forces were in the area. He alerted a squadron of Grumman F4F-2's to prepare for takeoff and to check out the fire. The Hornet would be moving toward that position and the squadron would be able to reach the fire and return with little trouble by daylight.

Captain Walker also alerted the marine Lieutenant Colonel on board to try to get a force of marines to the area as quickly as possible. He told him that he didn't yet know what was happening but the Japanese had some sort of mishap and it might be a window of opportunity for allied forces.

"At the very least I want to know what they were up to," was Paul Walker's last comment before he returned to his post.

It was five thirty when the squadron returned and in the briefing room they were told of an island on fire. There was moonlight so they could see the entire island but only the northern third was burning. It was the consensus that it was an oil fire of some sort and that it would burn for awhile. They didn't take any fire from below but there seemed to be a lot of activity on the beach.

The squadron commander asked permission to make a suggestion.

Given permission he said, "It is my opinion that they will abandon that island. If we get a couple of squadrons headed in that direction we can probably intercept a freighter or troop ship or both and hit these guys where it hurts. I don't know what caused that depot to blow up but let's take advantage of their misfortune."

Walker asked the commander if he would send marines to the island.

"Captain, I would wait till the fire dies down and send a group of leathernecks to find out what they were up to."

Walker thanked him and the squadron and dismissed them, telling them to get some rest. He liked the direct approach of his wing commander and felt that he would shortly be promoted.

A squadron of Douglas SBD Dauntless bombers was sent to the scene with two squadrons of Grumman Fighters. Walker hoped that they were not too late. For now all he could do was listen and hope. He did get the marines to agree to send a small force to check out the island.

Chapter 26

By mid morning all Japanese had left the island and were steaming north on a freighter toward safety and fighter protection. That was when they heard the first wave of bombers and fighters making a run at them. They had a few guns and relatively little protection and by the third pass the freighter was on fire and listing heavily to starboard. The bulk of the American planes headed for home and a few stayed to make sure the freighter was sunk.

After the freighter sank and the bombers were barely out of sight, five Zeros arrived on the scene looking for the enemy planes. It was, however, too late and all the Zeros could do was send a boat to pick up any survivors.

Late in the day a force of thirty marines landed on the east beach of the island. The fire didn't reach this spot and while much of the island was still burning, a light breeze from the east was keeping the smoke from the force. The marines were able to see the damaged remains of some of the oil drums on the edge of the field and rightly concluded that it was an oil depot. They sent a force to check out the circumference of the island by boat and the main force were looking for items that needed to be destroyed. The radio tent had been burned down and its contents a mess of molten metal. They dropped a grenade into the guts of both fork lifts for good measure and found a few rifles that they threw into the burning oil on the edge of the field. The warehouse tent was intact and they couldn't see anything of strategic value in the rows of supplies. The tents south of the warehouse were still standing but emptied of everything except bedding and personal possessions, hardly worthy of a grenade. No ammunition was found. They did blow up the generator.

The marines spent three hours on the island and concluded that it had been abandoned, that it had been an oil depot to supply submarines, that there was no living person on the island and what was left had no strategic value whatsoever. Before sundown they were ferried out to a destroyer and headed back to their convoy.

When Captain Paul Martin got a full report he thought that there was more to that little operation than was obvious. Would the Japanese use small islands like the one they had just abandoned to hide some of their operations and disperse their bases? If we didn't know it was there we wouldn't be interested in it. And since it was so small it wouldn't take much to supply an operation like that. He decided that intelligence should be brought in on what was known. What was not known was how a fire that large could have been started. No matter how it was started it was a blow to the Japanese submarine effort. How it happened would probably remain a mystery.

Chapter 27

Sometime in the night Buck woke. He was hungry and the smell of smoke was in the cave. It wasn't strong but it was there. He moved the rock and took a deep breath of fresh air. He hadn't realized how stale the air was until he smelled the fresh air.

Buck turned on the flashlight and looked at his leg. It was still swollen but not as bad as when he went to sleep. His watch told him it was six fifteen. And even though the sky was dark it must be morning. Which morning. Had he slept away a whole day? And while the red lines on his leg were still there, they weren't as angry. He had to have slept a whole day for such improvement. His fever seemed to have diminished and he was feeling hungry, very hungry. He had definitely missed a day. He would not be this hungry if he had just slept a few hours. He got his paddle and marked off a day. He wondered if it could have been two days that he had slept and was certain that he didn't sleep that long. That just wasn't possible.

He went outside and was met by an eerie stillness. The wind was blowing from the east, maybe even the southeast yet there was the smell of smoke all around. He took a few steps toward the ledge to see what was happening at the lagoon and realized that there was no sound of a generator and no lights. Was it possible that the Japanese had left? He did see the faint glow of some fires in the valley but all else was silent. He wanted to go down and see the damage he had caused but he wasn't certain that he was alone. It would be wise to wait for the sun to rise. Besides, he would not go down without breakfast. He was definitely hungry.

In the cave the bananas were ripe and Buck felt free to make a fire for some coffee. He ate one of his ration bars and made a note of the fact that he was running out of food. He wondered if he could steal some from the warehouse. He would have to get food.

He was finishing the last of his second cup when the sky showed the first signs of gray. And as with the sunset, the sunrise in the tropics is not a slow process. When the sun decides to rise, it does and when it sets it does what it has to do quickly. He didn't have to wait long before he could see a path to the valley.

The valley was like a picture out of hell, with trees smoking and fires burning everywhere. Everything in the valley and north of the valley was burned or burning. Everything south of the lagoon and the larger of the two hills was spared. Buck figured that the wind must have been blowing from the south or southeast. The hill would have funneled the wind toward the north. Nevertheless, he moved cautiously, suspicious that some Japanese might still be on the island. As he walked toward the lagoon he became convinced that he would not find anyone on the island. The island had been abandoned. Now maybe the Americans would come.

What he did find surprised and confused him. He saw a camel cigarette. In the dirt was a cigarette that had been crushed out. How would a Japanese soldier get a camel? Maybe he fought the marines in the jungle and after killing a GI he took his cigarettes. He would have had to keep them a long time. This bothered Buck and he wanted an answer. He strolled over toward the beach just east of the lagoon and saw the markings of landing craft to pick up or drop off men or supplies. Then he noticed the boot markings in the sand. American boots! Americans were here!

"Oh, God, I missed them," Buck yelled. "When did you come? Why didn't you find me? Are you coming back?" He fell to his knees in the sand and put his face in his hands. He couldn't believe it. The Americans had come and he was asleep.

These were the questions he voiced but there were so many more he wanted to ask. He knew he would not get an answer to any of them. Yet they had to be asked. As he continued to walk around the former Japanese camp his mind kept asking questions. He so wanted to know how the war was going both in Europe and the Pacific. He wanted to know about his family and what was happening back home. And what he wanted to know most of all was when he would be rescued from this island. He had the awful suspicion that it would not be any time soon.

He noticed that the motors on the two fork lifts had been blown apart. It looked like a grenade was dropped in the housing and they would not be used again. The radio tent was burned down and all the radio equipment was reduced to a melted pile of metal. The electric generator was also blown up and beyond repair.

Buck's meanderings took him to Chuck's place of business, the warehouse. The tent was intact as the wind was blowing from the south. He walked up and down the aisles and thought that at least the Japanese were nice enough to leave him some supplies. He found tarps of all sizes and shapes and unfolded several of them. He placed these over items that he valued and wanted to keep from getting wet if rain came through the tent. He assumed that there would be a few small holes caused by sparks. Toilet paper was one such item as was clothing and cardboard boxes of rations. Everything else could wait for another day.

He then continued on toward the tents just south of the warehouse. In the first tent he decided to sit down on a cot and realized that he hadn't slept in a bed in almost a month. He laid his head down on the pillow and knew immediately that he was going to take a rest. Besides his leg was throbbing and all this walking wasn't helping it to heal. And he did sleep. A deep sleep in which he was back home, playing baseball with some of his buddies. There was Leo, Guy and Buddy. They were playing touch football in the street in front of his house. And Alice was there too, watching. It was a nice dream but he was being pulled by the arm by some men and he didn't want to go. Bobby, Mickey and Alice were pleading with him to stay but the men wouldn't let go. Buck woke up with a start, frightened and confused. He sat on the edge of the bed and realized by the height of the sun and the shadow of the tent pole that it was afternoon.

Getting used to being alone again on the island required some adjustment. He was constantly looking before he moved and his eyes seemed to be busy checking out the tree line, the beach and all the areas he spied upon. He would have to learn to relax and not be like a high strung thoroughbred race horse. He had some very practical things that he had to think about.

Saying that he wanted to relax was more difficult to achieve than one would suspect. Every movement of the trees startled him as did the flight of a bird. He had told himself that he was alone on the island yet he searched the woods for soldiers and scoured the horizon for boats. Habits are not easily broken and that is as true for the habit of caution as it would be for the habit of smoking. Only time would break that habit.

He walked over to the beach and sat on the grass that separated the beach from the trees. In the sand he drew pictures of things he had to think about. He drew a tent, water, food, clothes and a raft. And since the tent was first he began to think that it might be nice to live in the tent instead of in the cave. But which one? All the tents to the north of the lagoon were burned to nothing. So it would have to be the ones south of the warehouse. He decided to have a look at all of them and pick out a tent that was located in heavy shade. Then he thought that he could use the tents on each side of the one he choose as supply tents, keeping things he wanted to be handy. As he walked back toward the tents, he realized that all this ambition would have to wait until his leg felt better. He stopped by the warehouse and found some fruit juice and some rations. Then he laid down on the cot in the first tent and fell fast asleep.

Chapter 28

Hunger woke Buck and he felt free for the first time to generously eat from the ton of rations in the warehouse. He also found some first aid supplies and moved them into his tent. He couldn't believe how different all of this freedom felt, not being cooped up in a cave with the enemy all around him.

Buck decided to find some soap and take a bath. He knew it would be good for his leg to be washed with salt water and he knew that he must be a mess from the dirt he crawled in and the soot all over everything. While he was in the warehouse he found some clothes that would replace his torn and filthy uniform. He remembered that he saw some civilian shirts in the personal effects left behind by the Japanese and he was certain that he could find something that fit. Before he walked the few steps to the beach he had gathered the essentials for a well dressed man.

After his bath and shave he dressed the leg wound and saw that it was much less angry, less swollen and the red lines were fading. He found some cream that looked like it was an antibacterial ointment and he spread that over the wound. He laid on a wide piece of gauze and generously covered the dressing with adhesive tape. While searching for the first aid material he also recognized a case of saki and brought a bottle and a cork screw back to his tent. He thought that the evening might be the perfect occasion for some sort of celebration.

Adjusting to this new life took time. All that week he continued to move items from the warehouse to the two tents on each side of his quarters. It gave him something to do that was not too taxing. He still didn't feel that he should climb the hill back to the cave but when he was ready he would return and get the items he needed. One of those items was the paddle that kept his calendar. He was using a book that Chuck left behind in his desk for the current days but left room for the month since the plane was shot down. Trying to locate a pen, he found boxes of them as well as boxes of notebooks of several sizes. He was definitely well supplied with stationery.

It was Friday, December 18th when Buck's leg showed major signs of improvement. He bathed every day, put on antibacterial ointment, dressed his wound and tried not to put too much weight on it when walking. An improvised crutch assisted him. Buck got rid of three of the cots in his quarters and made room for the desk once owned by Chuck. He found a small dolly which would probably do the job but he couldn't even consider all that lifting and pulling until his leg was better. But he liked the idea of having an office in his quarters.

This was the day to climb to the cave and retrieve the paddle and a few other items. He left the blanket and decided that he would leave what he would need should he ever be forced to hide. Water, food, candles and matches would remain in the cave. He planned on taking one of the rafts for use around the island. As best he could tell no other islands were in the area but maybe he could use the raft to fish. He could take the raft out a short way from the island as a diversion or for recreation. He began to consider rigging a sail and would study and learn where the coral was close to the surface and where he would have to avoid sailing.

On Saturday, December 19th Buck decorated a small tree near his tent for Christmas. This was the first time he realized that Christmas was so close. It would definitely have a different meaning this year. Being by oneself constantly is not a cause for joy. He was happy to be alive, to have blown up the depot which was meant to help supply the enemy and for the recovery of his health. Yet on an occasion like Christmas, memories of past holidays flooded his thoughts and it was difficult to keep from getting nostalgic and homesick over the event. He would celebrate the holiday as best he could.

Chapter 29

Lena made an appointment with an attorney the week before for three o'clock, Monday, December 21st. Miles Hart was a family friend and an attorney. He grew up across the street from Alice and the families knew each other from church. Martin was going to meet them at the attorney's office. Lena said that she would walk the mile or so to Hillside Avenue. The weather was sunny, cool but not cold.

Lena was rereading her letter for about the tenth time. The military sent Martin and Lena a check for Buck's death and back pay. Lena didn't want to accept it but Martin suggested that rejecting the check would only create problems and they would never be free of all of this. So Lena said that she would take the check if she could put it into an account for Buck for his use when he returned from war. Martin thought that was a good suggestion. Lena insisted on writing a letter to Buck and Martin encouraged her. The handwritten letter was read one more time.

December 21, 1942

Dear Buck,

A letter from the government arrived in the mail last week with a check for combat pay, insurance and death benefits. They have told us that your plane was shot down or lost at sea and there is no chance that you would have survived. We know that they are wrong and we don't want to take the money on false pretenses. So we decided to put the money into an account and to invest that money so that you will have a nest egg when you return home. We will tell your brother, Robert and sister, Maryann how you can access that account if we are not here for you.

Buck, we know that your experience in the war was memorable. We look forward to hearing all about those experiences. We want you to know that we have not for one moment believed that you didn't survive. I told you before you left home that you would return and every day I pray for you, not to you. We hope we are doing the right thing but we want you to know, above all else, that we never lost hope that you would return.

Love,
Mom and Dad

That afternoon, at the attorney's office, the letter was read. The attorney had several suggestions. He suggested that the letter stay just the way it was, handwritten and on personal stationery. He also suggested that an account be set up in Buck's name and that the money received be invested in four stocks which looked very promising and would be poised to take advantage of any postwar boom. He also suggested that Lena and Martin take possession of the account on January 1, 1951. In case neither of them were alive, Bobby and Mickey would take possession of the account. Miles Hart said that the time period would give Buck plenty of time to return from the war, if he was going to return. He also wanted the account to have a clear line of beneficiaries.

Lena and Martin had no objection except that Lena didn't like it when Miles said the phrase, "if he was going to return." He noticed the hurt and said that lawyers had to prepare for contingencies and that was why they were needed. He told them that he would draw up the papers and would send them for signatures, by mail. Where they had to sign would be clearly marked. Before he bought the stock he would call them. Then Miles Hart told Lena and Martin that there would be no fee for his services, that he wanted to do something for Buck and this would be his contribution to the war. They started to object but Miles put his hand on Lena's and told her it would be fine. He shook Martin's hand and told him that he appreciated their trust in him.

On the ride home in the car Martin told Lena that he was pleased with what they did and he too felt certain that Buck would return home. They spoke of what they would tell Bobby and Mickey. They arrived home for a cup of tea before supper. When Bobby and Mickey came in they were told of the arrangements and that it was being handled by Miles Hart with Sullivan, Kennedy and Hart Law Firm.

Mickey said, "That's nice, Mom." Bobby nodded in agreement.

Chapter 30

Christmas came like any other day. Buck had hoped that he would have found something to read but so far did not. As he went through the warehouse he would bring to his tent the items he would use daily. He stored in the next tent the items he might use in the near future. Then in the third tent he stored items that he might use occasionally.

As he celebrated the Birth of Christ he was keenly aware of how lonely it was on holidays like this one which called for being with family. He made it a special day by catching a fish and grilling it on a wood fire, by eating some of the fruit that he brought from the tree in the woods and by eating some ripe bananas. He also opened a bottle of saki and found that it was smooth when it was warm and leaving it in the sun for a while made it even better. He wasn't one to drink much alcohol but he did like having saki for special occasions.

Looking back over the past several weeks since the island oil depot blew up he realized that he had made a rather nice life for himself. He managed, with quite a bit of difficulty, to move the desk and chair into his tent. He updated the notes he kept on the paddle and wrote a full description of all that happened from the time he left the PBY to the present. He determined to keep a journal each evening of everything that happened each day.

He also set up a tarpaulin outside his tent that provided protection from the sun and rain and allowed him to cook outside. He moved the large life raft to a grove of mangroves and would take it out for a view of the island from the water. He also did some fishing when the spirit moved him. He found that he had become quite accurate spearing fish.

He also stocked the cave with items that would be useful if he had to hide. If the Japanese came they would probably eventually find him. He was quite certain that it wouldn't be for awhile. Water, food, a blanket, some clothes and a few items needed for use with the raft were neatly organized for a getaway. The smaller of the two rafts was kept in the cave and in an emergency could be used to escape the island and return to the small island he first found. He anticipated that he would have to make his escape at night. At least he had a plan should there be another invasion of his island.

It was late in the afternoon of Christmas when an idea crossed Buck's mind. Maybe he should look through the personal footlockers of the Japanese soldiers in search of reading material. He had moved each footlocker to the warehouse and piled them three high and covered the entire pile with tarpaulins. He started at one end and found mostly clothes. He made a note that if he was so inclined he could outfit himself quite well. As he searched each footlocker he saved valuable and useful items. He put watches and jewelry and knives in this pile. But mostly he found clothes. In several footlockers he found Japanese books. Finally, as he was running out of footlockers to check he found a treasure. He found a Bible in English and one in Japanese. He also found five western novels written by Zane Grey.

"What a Christmas," he said aloud. "What a Christmas!" He covered the footlockers and decided to complete that task another day. Now all he wanted to do was get to his desk and look at the books.

He said a prayer of thanks and whispered a thanks to the Japanese soldier who liked to read western novels. There was one called, "Forlorn River" and another titled, "Lighting the Western Stars." The other three were "The Border Legion," "Desert Gold" and "Wanderer of the Wasteland." He didn't know which one he would read first. He kept changing his mind until he decided that he was a wanderer and he would relate easily to "Wanderer of the Wasteland."

Buck was also pleased with his finding of the Bible. It wasn't the entire Bible, only the New Testament. When he lit his candle for the evening he read the Christmas story from St. Luke's Gospel. It did more to bring him back home than he could have possibly dreamed. He was transported around the world, back at St. Aidan's with Mom and Dad, Bobby and Mickey and listening to the Gospel and the sermon that followed. What a wonderful day and what a wonderful find. How thankful he was for all his blessings.

With those thoughts he ended his Christmas.

Chapter 31

The war in the Pacific continued and 1942 turned to 1943. Unknown to Buck, the Allies invaded New Guinea and the Japanese evacuated Guadalcanal. The war in the jungle continued as fierce as ever and after a year in which the Allies lost so many battles, they were now taking back some of the islands and territory lost to the Japanese. All that Buck knew was that he didn't know what was going on and he wanted to be back in the war. He was pleased to have destroyed the oil depot that the Japanese set up on the island but didn't like the damage that was done. He hoped that he had contributed to the war effort, in at least a small way. Maybe the plans the Japanese had for the depot were foiled and lives were saved.

Winter turned to spring with hardly any change in weather. The wind was more variable and would sometimes blow from the west. It was also a bit warmer and the sun was noticeably more overhead. Buck had found a good supply of the fruit that he was eating like bread and some other fruit that he liked but couldn't name. He also checked the berry bushes and frequently gathered enough for several evenings of desert. The bananas continued in good supply and the coconuts could always be counted on for a change of taste. Each day continued like the day before it.

What made life bearable was that Buck established a routine and kept to his timetable. He knew he didn't have to keep a routine but that it gave him a feeling that he was in charge. If the Americans landed tomorrow on his island they would find him healthy and fit. He swam almost every day, walked and ran on the beach, did stretching exercises and push ups and generally kept in shape. He could go into combat tomorrow if they asked him.

He also kept to a routine of reading the Bible each night and then meditating on what he just read. He didn't always understand the Epistles of St. Paul because he didn't always know the circumstances about which Paul was writing but he did understand the lessons Paul was imparting. He also wrote in his journal every evening and was close to filling up one notebook.

He felt that he was still a marine and that doing all these things was just part of being faithful. When he walked out at night he carried a flashlight in case he heard an American plane. He wasn't always sure he could tell an American plane but he knew for certain that he could recognize the sound of a Japanese plane. During the day he carried the mirror to notify any American plane should he see one. Yet he never saw or heard a plane.

Spring turned into summer and summer into autumn. The Allies were moving up the chain of islands toward the Philippines and on November 1st the U.S. Marines invaded Bougainville in the Solomon Islands. On November 20th U.S. Troops invaded the Gilbert Islands. The war was all around Buck but did not again touch this little speck in the corner of the Caroline Islands.

His second Christmas came and went and his longing to see his family and return to the marines remained at the top of his wishes and prayers. He was now very familiar with the island and many of the plants that somehow grew on the island. He never did find any animals probably because the island was too remote and in historical terms a young island. He finally got a good look at the blue bird that had so long eluded him. It looked like a dove and was about the size of a dove but was a deep blue. He didn't know the name of the bird but would never forget the beautiful sounds that the bird scattered over the island. These joys often reminded him of his parents and their attempts to teach him about the trees, birds and rocks and the beautiful things of nature all around him. His Mom especially loved the garden and helped him to appreciate flowers.

1944 was a great turning point in the war against the Japanese. The Japanese Naval Base at Truk, just a mere thousand miles away from Buck in the same Caroline Islands was destroyed on February 18th. All the Allied forces were moving closer and closer to the island of Japan, destroying the long supply lines the Japanese needed and getting closer to Iwo Jima. That island, within striking distance of Japan, was bombarded in November and on February 19, 1945 the invasion of Iwo Jima began.

Buck continued his ascetic life, missing his family terribly, wishing he was back fighting for his country.

Chapter 32

March 3, 1945 is the day listed when the U.S. and Filipino troops took Manila from the Japanese. Lena was listening to the radio, with fear and elation that the capital of the Philippines would soon be free. She was excited for her mother and her brother and sisters and all her relatives that they would no longer be under the control of the Japanese. Martin was called in to work on this Saturday and she was expecting him home before supper. Any time now. She was surprised to hear a heavy knock at the front door. She turned down the radio and answered the door.

Two policemen were standing on the porch. The taller of the two spoke.

"Mrs. Jones. May we come in?"

"Of course," Lena said as she understood what the next words were that he was about to speak.

"Your husband was shot this afternoon when he attempted to make a routine arrest. I'm sorry to inform you that he died on the scene, before an ambulance could get to him."

Lena sat down. She knew she would have to because she felt the room moving. The taller officer pointed to the kitchen and made a gesture like he was drinking a glass of water. The other took the clue and got Lena a glass of water. She didn't pass out but it was only because of will power and the cool water. When she recovered sufficiently, she thanked the officers.

The next three days were extremely difficult as they would be for anyone losing a spouse they loved. All the decisions were made a slight bit easier with Bobby at her side. He was only seventeen but he was acting so much more mature and he seemed to know the right things to say. He was also not moved by the undertakers attempts to sell services that were not wanted or needed. The Mineola Police Department also assigned a detective, a good friend of Martin's, to assist with the arrangements and Bobby found his advice very helpful.

The wake was Monday evening and a Requiem Mass was held at St. Aidan's Church on Tuesday morning and a full honor guard from the department was present. Father Sheridan, who knew Martin, spoke words that were true and comforting. After the final words were said at the cemetery and everyone expressed their condolences and said goodbye, Lena felt totally alone.

People had been invited back to the house and while she wished she hadn't invited them, she was actually pleased she had. These were friends, neighbors and fellow detectives. Some had known Martin a good portion of his lifetime. Lena felt the warmth and care they each had and realized that she would not be the only person to miss Martin. They could have gone home but wanted to be with her to celebrate Martin's life for just a while longer. She began to realize how important it was for her son and daughter to hear that they had a good and faithful father. The love of everyone at their home helped her. But she would miss him.

No one could have told Lena how alone she would feel when she climbed into bed without Martin getting ready or being in bed before her. She had gone to bed alone when Martin was on a case that required him to be out at night or when he was out of town attending a seminar. She knew at those times that he would be home eventually. But this was the only time since they said "I do," that she was truly alone. The knowledge that he would never return made the difference. Lena, at least for this one night, didn't know if she could live without him. Her tears stained her pillow.

Chapter 33

Buck knew nothing of the world events. It was as if he were asleep. The allies took Iwo Jima and landed on Okinawa. The British occupied Hong Kong. The war in Europe was over and the Nazis and Fascists were defeated. Japan was bombed and on August 6, 1945 the first atomic bomb was dropped on Hiroshima and three days later a bomb was dropped on Nagasaki. On August 14th the Japanese accepted unconditional surrender. Some Japanese continued to fight for another month. Yet the days for Buck were untouched by the final battles of war.

The new year was ushered in with a bonfire on the beach. It wasn't spectacular but it did two things. It was a celebration of sorts and it helped get rid of a lot of driftwood and debris that was piling up. Each day as Buck walked the beach he returned with an handful of wood for the celebration. Then at midnight on December 31, 1945 with a bottle of saki for a companion, the New Year was welcomed. He made a special plea that this would be the year he was rescued.

"Please, God, rescue me," was a very personal cry. He was surprised that he said it out loud. Then he said it again and blessed himself.

The only thing different about the next day was the headache that Buck was experiencing. He was able to find two aspirin in the first aid kit and got some relief. Possibly he was a little wiser. As Buck took stock of his New Year's resolutions he wondered what new resolution he could make. He read each of his five books five or six times already and read from the New Testament daily. He found that the Bible could be read over and over and would never get old.

He did set some new goals for his physical exercises and he made a resolution to spend more time preparing meals. He liked to cook a good meal and he found some food left behind by the Japanese that he had to learn how to prepare. Sometimes he wasn't even sure what the food was he was preparing. If he knew he figured that would help. The fish was good and fish and rice were always a good meal, especially when he found a vegetable to go with it all. On special occasions he opened a bottle of saki, usually only once a week. He figured at the rate he was drinking the saki it would last at least ten years. He didn't want to stay on the island that long even if the saki was good.

It was March 19, 1946 and Buck was deep in sleep. In his dream he was playing on the pier at Bar Beach near Roslyn, Long Island with Bobby and Mickey. It was low tide and they ran off the pier together, making a big splash. He could hear the splash. Then consciousness slowly returned and he realized that he was hearing voices and he actually heard a splash. He put on shorts and hurried barefoot to the beach. A sail boat was riding in the water about two hundred feet off shore. He saw a young man and a young woman in bathing suits jumping off the deck of the yacht and swimming to the ladder in the stern. A man and a woman were in the cockpit of the boat each with a cup in their hands. They didn't see Buck.

Buck watched from the shadows for a moment. They didn't look Japanese, nor did they look American. Then he saw a tricolor flag of red, white and blue on the stern. French! That was it, they were French. Buck was so excited he could hardly wait. He hurried to the life raft kept tied up to the mangrove trees and paddled out to the yacht.

They saw him and the two swimmers climbed on board. The man disappeared below and returned shortly with a pistol which he kept behind his back. They waited and watched as Buck paddled closer to them. When he got about twenty-five feet from the boat he stopped paddling and in his best high school French said, "Bonjour."

"Bonjour," was a weak reply from everyone.

"Je suis americain," said Buck.

"Bien," said the man. "Vouley-vous du café?"

"Oui," replied Buck starting to exhaust his vocabulary. "La Guerre?"

The man put away the pistol, extended his arm toward Buck and the young man reached for the painter to tie up the life boat. The man was saying something which was so fast and incomprehensible to Buck that he held up his hand and said, "Parlez-vous anglais?"

The young man said that he spoke English and his Mom and Dad understood it fairly well. His sister only spoke a little.

"Tell me about the war. Who won?"

They looked at each other and laughed. The mother explained something to the daughter and they all began to realize that Buck had been out of touch with the world for a long time.

"Reposez-vous, Monsieur," said the Father as he pointed to a spot in the cockpit. He asked his daughter to get a cup of coffee for their guest.

First of all, introductions were made. Buck found out that he was on the schooner, "Jours Heureux" translated, "Happy Days" with Anna and Pierre Renault. Their daughter was called Margarita or Rita and their son was Philippe. Philippe was eighteen and Rita was sixteen. Both were nicely tanned and attractive. Buck introduced himself as Corporal Martin Jones, with the United States Marines.

Philippe told Buck that the Allies had won the war both in Europe and the Pacific. He explained that the war has been over for half a year when the Americans dropped two bombs on Japan that killed so many people that Japan knew it was futile to resist. As Philippe explained, tears came to Buck's eyes. He tried to push back the emotion but all this news was too much. Pierre came over and put an arm about him and told him to cry. And Buck did.

Finally the tears changed to tears of joy and then to laughter. What happiness! Buck's heart was bursting with the excitement of such good news and being able to share all his emotion. For most of the morning he listened and asked questions and got caught up on what was happening in the world.

Buck found out that the Renaults were taking a year to explore the South Pacific, mainly Micronesia. The trip was planned years before when the children were much younger but the war interrupted their plans. They were teachers on Iles Wallis, an island owned by the French near Samoa and they were taking a sabbatical. They told Buck that they would get him to a port that could notify the Americans that he was alive.

Buck asked them if they would like to see his home. He knew that he had a few items that he would like to take with him when he left his island. First and foremost were his journals. Just about everything else was expendable. He showed the Renaults around his campsite, his tent with the desk and chair and the cooking area outside the tent. He showed them his supply of saki and told them to take as much of it as they wished as well as any other items that they saw. They took two boxes of saki for the boat and Philippe put it in their dingy and motored out to the yacht. Then he returned.

Buck told his story and explained why the northern end of the island was burned. Even though the taller trees were black because of the fire, there was a good growth of smaller bushes, ferns and undergrowth. The island was returning to the way it was before the invasion and fire. He told of the cave where he lived when the Japanese were on the island. Philippe said he would like to see it and Rita said that she would like to join them.

The three of them hiked up the hill to the cave. They were in great shape and hardly raised a sweat when they arrived near the cave. Buck told them that they were within fifteen feet of the entrance and asked them to find the opening. They were standing right in front of it and with the new growth and the rock rolled against the entrance they couldn't see his cave. He showed them how to enter and the three crawled into the cave. There was a flashlight there and while the battery was a bit weak it gave them enough light to see the entire room. He explained that all the survival gear was stowed here in case the Japanese returned and he had to hide. This time it would be much more difficult because they would know he was there.

When they returned to the camp the Renaults were walking along the beach. Pierre said something to Philippe and he told Buck that it might be wise to get to the yacht and make plans to see where they could go to return Buck to the Americans. All Buck needed was some clothes, his boots, toiletries and his journal. He looked about his camp, said a silent goodbye and walked to the beach. Philippe had already ferried Rita and Anna in the small dingy to the yacht and was returning to pick up Pierre and himself.

On board they looked at maps of Micronesia. It was as if the island was equidistant from everywhere. Pierre and Philippe plotted and both seemed to agree that it would be best to head for Palikir. It was a fair sized port and from there the Americans could be contacted. It would take the rest of this day, all of the next and if the winds remained steady they would arrive on Thursday, the 21st. It was agreed.

Chapter 34

The pains were coming more frequently now, usually about once a day. At first it was just discomfort like heartburn but more recently she had numbness in her shoulder and in her jaw. On Monday, the 18th of March, she called Doctor Rhodes and asked for an appointment. She didn't want to tell the nurse what it was about and did not indicate any urgency about her wanting to see him. So the nurse told her to come in on Thursday, the 21st at nine o'clock. She marked it on the calendar in the kitchen and went about her work.

Lena was taking the garbage out to the street when the pain hit her. It didn't last long as she was dead before she fell to the ground. It was Beatrice Segner next door who noticed her lying on the driveway. She ran to her side and immediately felt the artery in her neck for a pulse. She knew it was too late. Flo Theme across the street saw the two of them and came running.

"Lena's dead, Flo," said Beatrice.

"Should I call the police?" asked Flo.

"Yes, let them decide how to handle this."

Within a few minutes the police arrived, took statements from Beatrice and Flo and called for an ambulance to take the body. Beatrice explained that Bobby and Mickey were in Mineola High School and that Lena had no family of her own in the States but her deceased husband, Martin, had a brother who lived in New Hyde Park. She wasn't sure of his first name but he was a Jones and he worked for the Fire Department in Floral Park. The police thanked her for the information.

With help from Lena's brother-in-law, Larry, Bobby and Mickey survived the ordeal of losing their mother. Larry and his wife, Carol, had no children and always wanted a child. They didn't hesitate to offer their home to Bobby and Mickey. Both were pleased with the offer as they liked their Aunt Carol and Uncle Larry. Larry told Bobby and Mickey that he would do all he could to settle everything for them. He was happy that Lena had a will and he told them that his job would be a lot easier because of that. He was extremely pleased that his name was listed as the executor of the will. After the funeral there would be insurance, funeral expenses, clearing up of any debts, the selling of the house and financial arrangements for both Bobby and Mickey. Bobby was planning to go to the University of Pennsylvania on a partial baseball scholarship in the fall and he would use his share to pay some of his college expenses. Mickey would still be in high school for two more years so any money would be put into a trust account.

Bobby told Larry about the account that Mom and Dad set up for Buck with their attorney, Miles Hart. Bobby knew that it would still be several years before that money could be touched, based on Mom and Dad's wishes. Bobby explained that his Mom had believed that Buck was alive. This was her way of telling Buck that she knew that he would survive. Miles Hart didn't make fun of her notion but thought that a time limit should be put on the account as to when it could be dispersed. That date was January 1, 1951, if Bobby remembered correctly. Mickey said that she though that date was correct. Larry said that he would check on the account.

Alice was at the Requiem Mass for Lena with her mother. She had married two years before and was expecting their first child. She had always liked Lena and she thought that one day Lena would be her mother-in-law. That was not to be. Lena understood that she had to get on with her life and she held no resentment that Alice didn't share her belief that Buck was alive. How could she? They remained friends and Alice would occasionally stop by the house to spend a few minutes with Lena. Lena liked that and had great affection for Alice. They would always be friends.

It was difficult for the children to bury their mother. They loved her very much and knew how devoted she was to them. Mickey was able to keep it all together until the gravesite. Carol held her and gave her the strength to continue. When Mickey returned home, she wanted to sleep for a bit and after an hour was almost back to her old self. Buck's name was mentioned and more than once someone said that Lena truly died of a broken heart. The fact that Buck wasn't home was always in Lena's thoughts. Yet, not for a moment did she waver in her belief that he would survive. Everyone at the house knew what Lena believed but they kept their opinions to themselves.

Helena Jones was buried on Thursday, March 21, 1946 next to her husband, Martin.

Chapter 35

True to their word they reached Palikir on Thursday, but later in the afternoon than they had wished. Pierre and Philippe went to the customs house, showed their passports and explained that this gentleman was an American marine who was found alive on an island. The Americans were held in high esteem for liberating the Micronesians from the Japanese. Everyone was most anxious to be of service. Several of the authorities had ideas and it seemed that everyone was talking at once. Finally, one man stepped forward and said in English, "Do you want us to contact the Americans for you?"

"Yes," replied Buck.

"I will contact them. It may take a little bit of time but you can walk around outside if you wish. We have a lovely town," he told them.

They walked up the street, looking in the windows. As Buck had no money he knew he couldn't buy anything. They didn't go far and in about fifteen minutes they were waved back to the customs office.

"You are to stay at the Palm Tree Hotel up the street," said the customs officer. "Tomorrow a plane will land here and take you back to an American Base. All expenses will be paid for by the American who comes for you. You can charge anything you wish. Let me escort you to the hotel and tell management that you are a guest."

Pierre and Philippe accompanied Buck to the hotel. The customs officer explained everything to the hotel manager and Buck was given a key to a room. Pierre and Philippe said that they would go back to the boat and Buck said that he would go with them as he wanted to say goodbye and thank both Anna and Rita. Buck made sure that he got their address and he told them that he would write a long letter telling them about his life at home and what he found when he got there.

Buck told everyone how thankful he was for them to sail him to Palikir and to help him get acclimated to this new life. His happiness for the last three days was unlike anything he had ever experienced. He was truly happy and looking forward to returning to his family in New York. He told them to enjoy the saki and to think of him when they had a glass. He watched them motor out of the harbor and saw the jib and mainsail fill with the ocean breeze and disappear behind a spit of land and hill that enclosed the port. He walked back to his hotel, feeling a bit lost after having spent three wonderful days with very nice people.

The room provided to Buck was very luxurious and much larger than he expected. After a shower he realized that he needed some clothes. He went down stairs in his old shorts and spoke with the desk clerk, who called the manager. The manager told him to go to any store he wished and to buy what he needed. They would bring the bill to the hotel and the American officer would pay it when he came.

So Buck got some nice pants, a shirt, shoes and socks, a toothbrush, toothpaste, and a razor. He also got a small bag in which to carry these items. His journals were foremost on his mind. He left his old clothes with the storekeeper. While he was out he decided he needed a haircut and so got his hair trimmed. Till now he had to cut off his hair with his knife and it made him appear like a savage. He felt that he now looked presentable.

In the hotel restaurant there was a buffet for supper. Everything looked so good and attractive that it was difficult to make a choice. He choose steak and shrimp. When he sat at his table the waiter said just two words. "Red, white?" He figured that he was asking what kind of wine he wanted so he said that he wanted red. The waiter returned with a half carafe of wonderful red wine. At the end of the meal the waiter returned with a tray full of deserts. Buck felt too full and so refused but did finish the rest of the wine before returning to his room. Tired, satisfied with a wonderful meal and in anticipation of returning to the world of the military and to the world of his family, he quickly fell asleep.

Chapter 36

He couldn't believe that it was ten fifteen when he awoke. The wine must have been the culprit. He went down to breakfast and got wonderful food from the buffet table. The coffee was superb and he consumed a second cup. He checked at the desk and was told that no one had arrived as yet for him. So he strolled the main street. He found a western book in English in one store window and decided to buy it. All he had to do was point to the hotel and the storekeeper knew what to do. It was a Zane Grey that he hadn't read. He returned to the hotel and was sitting in the lobby when a marine walked in.

"Corporal Jones," he bellowed. Since Buck was the only person sitting in the lobby he speculated correctly.

"Yes, Sir."

"I'm Captain Les Rogers. I've come to collect you and bring you to our base on Wake Island," he said as if he was a mile away from Buck. Then he realized that the captain was in the habit of having to shout over the roar of the plane motor.

"Captain, I have a few items in the room I need to get. Then I'll be ready."

"I'll pay the bill while you're collecting your things. We have a taxi outside."

After getting the small duffel bag, they took the taxi to the dock. There was a PBY sitting just as pretty as could be next to the dock where the yacht was tied up yesterday. A First Lieutenant was standing guard over it. He was introduced to First Lieutenant Harold Harding. A few minutes later they were taxiing to the center of the harbor. With a lot of noise and a fairly long takeoff the plane was eventually free of the water and climbing toward the clouds.

"We're going to be flying for a good long time. We were up at three this morning and so one of us will probably be in the sack. We'll be in the air for about seven hours or so. You know your way around a PBY so just make yourself at home," said Captain Rogers.

Buck sat in the pilot's seat when the Captain was taking a nap and the co-pilot's seat when the Lieutenant was taking a nap. He also got up frequently to take a walk and view the ocean from the waist blisters and to play host when coffee was needed. He read some of his new book but on his mind was the fact that he was going home.

It was almost midnight when they landed on the runway of Wake Island. Buck went with the Captain and Lieutenant to the barracks and was assigned a bed. Sleep followed almost immediately. Morning came quickly and Buck was surprised to see a military uniform on the chair next to his bed. He was even more surprised when it fit him perfectly. He dressed and went to breakfast. He was then escorted to the base commander's office. He introduced himself as Colonel Ashley Hickey and he welcomed Buck back to civilization. He told him that he was going to be debriefed. They were going to ask him a lot of questions and it was important for him to tell them everything as truthfully as he could remember it. Another officer would be there in a moment and a recorder would take down what he was about to say.

"Sir, do you mind if I run back to the barracks to get my journal?" asked Buck.

"You've kept a journal?"

"Yes, Sir."

"How complete is it?"

"Except for the first few weeks when I marked the dates and events on a paddle, I wrote in the journal every day. I did write about those days as soon as I could after I got a journal and pens. It's very complete."

"By all means, get the journal," said the base commander. "Let me call you a jeep."

When Buck returned he was introduced to a Major Arnold Wright and a stenographer, Corporal Jennifer Adams. The base commander, Colonel Hickey, asked to see the journal and was surprised that there were three journals. Except for the first few pages which were written as a narrative, each day was clearly labeled with the day of the week and the date. As the Colonel continued to read he thought that a debriefing was unnecessary and he said so. He asked Major Wright to look at the journals and see if these would answer any questions that he might have. The two men continued reading for a few minutes. Major Wright asked if Buck was certain that the entire crew were blown up with the airplane. Buck answered that he was. Did Buck know the name of the island where he spent the last three and a half years? Buck answered that he did not. Did he have the address of the French family that rescued him. He said that he did and he gave them the address of the Renaults.

Colonel Hickey told Buck after the Major and Corporal had left that he was going to recommend that Buck receive a medal for his acts of courage. He said that after further review of the journals and confirmation by the Renaults of the rescue he would put in for back pay. If it was Buck's desire he would arrange for a discharge and trip back to New York as soon as possible. He said it was.

Buck asked the Colonel to return the journals when he was finished as he didn't want to leave without them. The Colonel said that he would make copies and give him the original within the hour.

"Do you have any other requests?" asked the Colonel.

"Yes, Sir. I'd like to notify my parents that I am alive," replied Buck.

"I'll get someone on it right away. We'll have to go by short wave to Hawaii and patch you through from there. It will take some time. Go back to the barracks and I'll send someone for you when we get through. Let me get the information."

Buck gave the Colonel the information and telephone number and realized that it would be another six hours before it was morning in New York. He told the Colonel that he would be patient and that he was ready to fly back to the States when a plane was available.

"Hold on." The Colonel had something in mind and said that Buck should go to the barracks and get his gear and he would send someone for him in a few minutes. He shook his hand and got back on the phone.

Ten minutes later a jeep arrived at the barracks and a private first class called his name and told him that a plane was warming up as they were speaking. It was a Brewster F2A Buffalo that was warming up by the tower and the private walked him over to the plane. A flight jacket and parachute were on the wings, waiting for Buck. Moments later the plane was racing down the runway and he was on his way to Hawaii. The flight was not too comfortable as Buck was sitting behind the pilot and it was noisy in the cockpit. He didn't care since he was getting home a lot faster than expected and that had to count for something.

In Hawaii, he was discharged later that day. Transportation to New York was finally arranged. He asked if he might call the States and his parents. They said they would try. Later in the day they told Buck that when they got through, the phone would ring but there was no answer.

They would try again. The rest of the day and evening the answer was the same. No one was answering. Buck was told to get a good night's sleep and he would fly back to the mainland in the morning.

The next morning he was awakened and told that a cargo plane was leaving in a half hour. He quickly dressed, had breakfast, grabbed his small duffle bag and was driven by jeep to the airfield runway and the plane. There were a half dozen soldiers and a lot of cargo going to the States. How nice it was to be going home even if it was in the hold of a cargo plane and he would be sitting on a jump seat.

It was late in the afternoon when they arrived in San Diego as they lost four hours going east. Buck had to wait an hour but there was another cargo plane going to Fort Dix. Buck was eager to go even if it meant flying all night. In the hour he was in San Diego, a civilian secretary tried making a call to his parents and had the same results. No one answered the phone.

On the plane Buck kicked himself for not calling Alice. Maybe she could tell him what was happening and why they weren't answering. He was sorry that he didn't call her. The plane flew all evening and all night and landed just as the sun was rising on Monday, March 24th. He got a ride to New York City on the military bus and with his military orders got a ticket to Williston Park on the Long Island Rail Road. The colonel had given him forty dollars from his own pocket when he was on Wake Island and he almost refused, thinking he wouldn't need it. But he had to buy breakfast when he reached Pennsylvania Station and would need money for a cab when he arrived at the station. It might be a while before his back pay arrived.

Exhausted but happy to be going home he fell asleep for about thirty minutes from New York to New Hyde Park. Then with eager anticipation he got up and went to the door between the cars and waited for the train to arrive at his station. When he stepped off the train in Williston Park he truly felt like he was home.

Chapter 37

He didn't have to tell the cabby where Henry Street was. That surprised Buck.

"Did you see any action?" the cabby inquired.

"Yeah, some."

"How come you're getting home now?"

Buck decided not to get into the whole story and so told the cabby that he was detained after the war for a while. He told him he was a radar operator and his services were needed. That seemed to satisfy him.

They arrived at 23 Henry Street and Buck paid the cabby and with his little duffle bag walked up to the door. This was a moment he had dreamed of a hundred times. The door was locked. He tried the doorbell. No one answered. He waited and still no one came. He looked next door and didn't see anyone and then the door across the street opened and Flo Theme asked him what he wanted.

"Mrs. Theme. It's me, Buck. I'm looking for my Mom."

"Buck. I don't believe it. I don't believe it. Come over here and let me give you a hug," she gushed.

He did as he was asked even though he wasn't too pleased to be gushed over.

"Where's my Mom? Has she moved?"

"Buck, I don't want to be the one to tell you but your Mom died last week. And your father died a year ago. He was shot making an arrest. Your Mom had a heart attack last Monday morning taking out the garbage. Mrs. Segner found her and I called the police. It was so sad."

Buck felt weak and asked to sit on Mrs. Theme's steps. Tears were in his eyes and he was fighting to keep from crying like a baby.

"Where's Bobby and Mickey?"

"They are with your Uncle Larry. I'll give you his number in New Hyde Park. I have his work and home number."

"Maybe I'll just call Alice. I'm anxious to see her."

"Buck," Flo said, "She may not be anxious to see you." She hesitated, then continued. "She was married two years ago and is expecting some time soon. Talk to Bobby and Mickey. They can tell you more. That's all I know."

In the four years since this adventure started, a lot had changed. Buck knew that things wouldn't be the same but this was staggering. He was having difficulty absorbing all the news and so far all of it was bad. Flo sensed this and told Buck to come in, have a cup of tea and some lunch and she would get in touch with Uncle Larry or Aunt Carol. He didn't want to but the offer sounded too good to be refused.

When Larry got on the line, Buck asked about Mickey and Bobby. He was assured that they were doing fine. He told Larry where he was and Larry said that he would be off from work in a bit and would come and get him. In the meantime, Mrs. Segner came across the street and gave Buck a genuine warm welcome. Then she said, "This hug is from your mother."

In about an hour Larry drove up in front of the Jones' house and knocked on Mrs. Theme's front door. After thanking both ladies for their kindness and promising to visit them soon and tell them about his experience he went with Larry to New Hyde Park. His Aunt Carol met them at the door and gave Buck a warm welcome. He told them that he had already eaten lunch and so they sat down in the living room to talk. How free he felt to tell his Aunt and Uncle all that had happened. Even so he knew it would take many sessions before he could tell it all.

Larry and Carol told Buck to make himself at home and over the next few days he would learn all there was to learn. When Mickey came home from school she couldn't believe her eyes.

"Buck," she screamed. "You made it home. Mom always knew you would." She dropped her books, ran over and gave Buck a big hug and he spun her around lifting her feet from the floor. "Buck, this is wonderful. I can't believe it."

"Mickey, I can't believe how you've grown. You're a young lady."

"Buck, you didn't think I'd remain a little tomboy the rest of my life?"

"No, I'm just experiencing shock at all the changes. I just didn't prepare for these things," Buck confessed.

It was Mickey's thought that they lost Mom last week and gained Buck this week. She told him how Mom never gave up the idea that he was alive and a hero. "Were you a hero, Buck?"

"I don't see myself as a hero. I was the only one who survived when our plane ditched in the ocean and I spent three years sitting on an island not knowing if we were winning or losing."

"Buck, you're not telling everything. Before the next few days pass I want to hear all about your years as a marine," Mickey told him.

Buck asked about Bobby and found out that he had baseball practice. He guessed that he could wait another hour.

"Buck," Larry asked. "Want a beer?"

"Yeah, that would be nice. I haven't had one since I've returned to civilization."

It was cold and crisp and it made Buck feel like he was home.

When Bobby walked into the house he saw Buck but wouldn't believe his eyes. He dropped his books and glove on the chair and stepped forward, almost afraid that it wasn't true.

"Buck. Buck, is that you?" He stepped up to his brother and the two stood eye to eye. Then they hugged each other as if they would never see each other again. Something which almost happened.

It was a wonderful evening and promises of better days ahead. Buck regretted that he wasn't home a week or so earlier but Mickey was most practical when she said that if he had come home several weeks ago Mom would have had a heart attack for certain. Larry and Carol told Buck about Martin's death trying to bring in a suspect for questioning. Before going to bed, Larry told Buck that the money paid by the government for his death and some back pay and insurance was in an account and was administered by Miles Hart. He said that tomorrow was soon enough to talk about these things.

Epilogue

It took about a week for Buck to feel like he was getting a hold on his new life. With Larry, he visited Miles Hart and read his mother's letter. It was as if God had spoken to her directly because she believed that he was alive when there was absolutely no rational reason to hold that position. And his father went along with his Mom because her belief was so strong.

Buck also told Miles and Larry that any money realized from the sale of the house and from his parent's savings and insurance should go to Bobby and Mickey. They would need the money for college. Besides, according to Miles Hart the four stocks that he invested in were doing very well. He invested in stocks that would do well when the boys came home from war. He choose Ford, AT&T, IBM and Mobile Oil. In a few days Buck would also receive back pay from the government.

The call to Alice was easier than he thought it would be. After he got over the shock of Alice's marriage and pregnancy, he realized that she was acting sensibly. No one but his Mom had a direct line to the Almighty and was certain he was alive. Once Alice accepted Buck's death it was her job to get on with her life. That's all she did. Buck made sure that Alice knew that he had no hard feelings and wished her love, happiness and joy with the new baby. It was a nice conversation and they parted as good friends.

Buck had to call the marines and give them his new address. There was a message for him to call a Lieutenant Colonel Paul Walker. Colonel Walker asked Buck some questions about his role in blowing up the oil depot on the island in the Caroline Islands. He had a name for the island that Buck had never heard of and promptly forgot. Buck told him about his journals and the fact that he left a copy of the journals with Colonel Ashley Hickey on Wake Island. He told Buck that he would recover the journals from Wake as they would fill in a few holes in what actually had happened. He also said that as the result of the blowup of the oil depot the Japanese submarines were deprived of a refueling base and after the Allies cut off Rabaul they were hurting for a place to refuel. They often had to take precious weeks to return to Japan. That was a crippling blow to Japanese submarine superiority in the Pacific. He also told Buck that marine bombers caught up with the ship that evacuated the island and destroyed it that same day.

It was a month later when Buck received a check in the mail for back pay, made out to Sergeant Martin Jones along with a commendation and a medal. There was a write up about Buck's story written by the marines and Buck was asked to sign a release to allow them to send it to the newspapers. Larry, Carol, Bobby and Mickey all encouraged him to do so. Shortly after that a flattering story appeared in the Long Island newspaper, Newsday and in the New York Times.

Buck handled many requests to tell his story at civic gatherings and at high schools in the area. He became good at public speaking, maybe because he was telling a story that had a profound effect on his life. He loved reading to his audience the letter his mother wrote after she was told that he was killed. His story was her story and the love and faith she lived. He was the marine who believed in being always faithful and his Mom was the epitome of faithfulness. He did not doubt for a minute that she was the reason he made it back home from the war.

About the Author

William F. Kelly has been a writer of technical and business articles for the major portion of his life. He has a Master's Degree in Education and has taught High School English. His experience has been in the fields of government, education, religion, training and construction. His life is varied and interesting, allowing him to bring a wealth of experience to the written page. Not only has he traveled extensively throughout Europe, South America, Australia, New Zealand and the United States but has lived in such diverse places as the Arctic, Europe, New York and Texas. This is, however, his first published novel. He is presently retired and devotes his time to painting, gardening and writing. He resides with his wife in Birmingham, Alabama.

Printed in the United States
37618LVS00006B/415-513